LOVE AND THE LIBRARY

LAUREN CONNOLLY

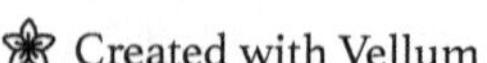 Created with Vellum

1

HANNAH

THESE SLOW-AS-HELL sorority girls need to get out of my way before I mow them down. If you want to stop and chat with your friends, go ahead, but not in the middle of the walking path. I have to sidestep into the grass to dodge around their giggling group. Once clear of them, I push my legs to the highest level of speed that can still be considered walking.

I'm going to be late.

Why did my professor think it was okay to lecture five minutes past the end of class? Doesn't he know some of us have places to be?

My heavy backpack smacks against my spine as I power-walk across campus.

If I wasn't in such a rush, I might take a moment to enjoy the warm spring day. The groundhog was wrong because it's only mid-March, and the temperature is kissing upper sixties. I actually took the extra five minutes needed in the shower to shave my legs this morning, so I could pull out a set of my favorite tweed shorts. The sun soaks deep into my skin, baking my bones.

This is one of the reasons I decided to come South for college. Not that Virginia is tropical or anything, but the winters run away sooner than in the frozen hell of Rochester. It is most definitely *not* shorts weather there right now. Mom is probably digging her car out of a foot of snow at this exact moment.

So, normally, I would be strolling along, breathing in the thick, humid air carrying the sweet scent of newly blooming flowers and the pungent tang of freshly spread mulch. I'd smile up at the sky, where wisps of clouds did little to block out the great expanse of rich blue.

But it's Tuesday afternoon, which means there's no time for dawdling.

The library looms up tall before me, built in an almost Gothic style with its heavy gray bricks and rounded corners. Inside though, it's a lot like other university libraries. Computer stations everywhere, colorful furniture, front desk staffed with helpful student workers.

I blow past them. Well into my second year here, I know exactly where I'm headed.

The elevator decides to work in slow motion, rudely ignoring my insistent pressing of the Door Close button. Finally, the silver doors slide shut, and I ascend at a crawl.

"Come on. Come on," I mutter to myself, a silent prayer that I'm not too late.

My shoulders ache from the weight of my backpack, a physical reminder of all the homework I need to get done before my eight a.m. class tomorrow. Each semester, the workload grows heavier, as if the professors enjoy the idea of me struggling to maintain my academic scholarship.

I haven't let them break me—yet. All I need is a quiet, comfortable place to focus. Give me that, and I'll scale the mountain of work like the badass I am.

A chime sounds, and the doors inch open. I don't wait for

them to finish before shoving through and jogging forward, no one around to judge me. At least, that's what I hope.

But when I turn the corner, I find all my speedy efforts were in vain.

Across the way, sitting in a casual slouch like he owns the place, is my nemesis. The sight of him there—his long fingers fiddling with a lock of his disheveled brown hair; his disinterested, round eyes tripping over the words in the textbook propped in his lap—brings on a wave of anger that slides from my now-hot cheeks down to my purple-painted toes.

The gall of him to show up here again and take what should be mine.

The Chair.

Search this entire library, the whole campus even, and no study spot will compare to The Chair. It's an old leather piece with a wide, single cushion and low, rounded armrests. So many options exist for sitting in it. All of them perfect in their own way. Study late into the night, and you'll never get an achy back or sore neck because you can shift and turn and lounge in all positions.

But this study spot does not dominate all others based on The Chair alone. The placement also needs to be taken into account. With the seat pushed up against a wide window, the sitter can unlatch a section to enjoy a refreshing breeze. The clear panes of glass let in plenty of natural sunlight, making it easy to read over notes during the day. But don't worry if the sun sets because a tall lamp stands just behind The Chair. Pull its little dangling chain, and the perfect amount of light spills out from under the shade.

Anxious about where to place all your excess books? Don't let that bother you another minute. Sitting at the exact right distance in front of The Chair is a heavy wooden coffee table, its surface happy to support bags, books, and snacks.

And apparently, feet, which my nemesis has propped up at the moment.

With him looking so cozy, my guess is, he won't be packing up anytime soon. Still, I don't want to miss my chance if he does. So, I settle for a spot at a table that's within eyeline of The Chair.

Sitting down on the wooden seat is like expecting to get handed an ice cream cone but instead realizing you're clutching a head of raw broccoli.

I can feel the disappointed grimace twisting my lips. So much for studying in comfort.

As my butt complains, I shoot another withering glare at my nemesis. That's how I refer to him in my head—partly because he is, but also largely because I don't know his actual name.

At the very end of my freshman year, I discovered The Chair. Coming back in the fall, I decided to take up residence in the newfound study haven as often as possible.

Turns out I wasn't the only one with this idea. And so began the unspoken battle with the mystery man.

If I had to give him a name, I'd go with Lucifer. Because every time I see him, I wish he'd go to hell.

The amount of brain power I allot to my hostility toward him is probably unhealthy. In contrast, I doubt he even realizes I exist or that this silent competition is something I plan my schedule around.

But who can blame him? If I had The Chair, I wouldn't take notice of the surrounding world either.

———

NATHAN

She's back.

The second the elevator let out its little arrival ding, I knew it was a matter of seconds before she came around the corner. And I was right.

Pretending to be absorbed in my textbook, I watch out of the corner of my eye as she fights to contain her rage at finding me in The Spot.

Her lips press tightly together, and her slim black brows angle down dramatically. But the best part is when, apparently unable to stifle her anger completely, she stomps her foot. The sight is adorable.

And it's not the first time I've seen it.

Last semester, there were a few times I found The Spot filled, so I grumbled to myself and wandered away to some other less impressive chair. This is the best seat in the library, what with it being so far away from foot traffic, having access to a window, and sitting next to a low table, perfect for resting my feet on. No wonder other students want The Spot as badly as me. But over time, I came to realize whenever I missed out on it, the person in the old leather armchair was the same girl.

After I noticed that fact, it wasn't long before I became aware of her arrival when I was already sitting down. One day, I glanced up at the sound of someone approaching, and there she was, glaring at me. I pretended not to see her, dropping my gaze back to my book, but by the clomp of her heavy footsteps, I got the impression she'd left in a huff.

A girl her size wouldn't make so much noise unless she was slamming her feet down with purpose.

From that moment on, I never overlooked the arrival of my contender even if she never realized I was watching her.

It's become a sort of game for me. First, will I beat her to The Spot? Then, if I do, the question is, will Shorty get mad?

I bet she'd hate me even more if she knew about my secret nickname for her. We haven't stood next to each other, but I'd be surprised if she cleared five feet. Despite lacking in the height department, she's not what I'd call petite. Shorty has some muscle on her arms and legs. And that butt would probably be a generous handful.

Today, I'm able to fully admire it. That pair of shorts grips her hips in all the right ways. I've never really understood the high-waisted trend, but on Shorty, I'm starting to get it. Her waist is more defined, and I glance teases of her rib cage above her shorts and below the T-shirt she's cut the bottom off of. Over the shirt, she's thrown on a blazer, like she hasn't decided if she wants to be casual or professional.

Over the winter, she wears a similar get-up but jeans instead of shorts. I prefer this. Her bare, golden legs are a nice springtime treat.

I look my fill while appearing to keep my eyes on the page in front of me.

After her angry foot stomp, Shorty huffs out a heavy breath before stalking over to a nearby table. Nowhere near as comfortable as The Spot though. I almost feel bad for her gorgeous behind sitting on that hard wooden chair, missing out on the chance to sink into the well-worn leather I'm currently sprawled across. But I don't let the guilt stick around.

If she wanted The Spot, then she should've shown up earlier. And I'm not enough of a gentleman to give it up. I've already had to vacate my dorm room, which is supposed to be my home away from home. Freshman and sophomore year, it felt that way. But my roommate seemingly transformed into a different person over the summer, and his new extracurricular activity means I can't ever count on the place being quiet.

Across the way, her eyes continue to burn into me like death rays as she pushes aside her curtain of silky black hair. I don't mind the heat though, seeing as how I have a nice breeze floating in from the open window to cool me down.

Shorty obviously chose her seat in hopes that I'd be up and out soon and she could swoop in.

I'm tempted to meet her angry gaze with a smirk before calling out to her to get comfortable because I have no plans to relocate.

Instead, I ignore her and get back to my textbook, keen on finding how long my competitor will hold out.

2

HANNAH

Lucifer didn't move more than an inch. For two hours.

Does the guy not have a bladder? Or a life?

I guess I'm not one to talk, seeing as how I've sat there just as long. Also, I don't have what most college students would consider "a life" either. For that, I'd need some friends.

Everyone told me making connections would be no problem in college. Join a club. Go to parties. Meet up with classmates.

Well, the clubs I checked out were full of drama and power plays, the parties were horror shows of drunken jocks with roaming hands, and the classmates I studied with seemed to be put off by some aspect of my personality.

I know I can be intense at times. I try my best to tone it down around strangers.

But still, at least I'm not the devil incarnate.

Goose bumps skitter over my skin as the evening air cools without the sun around to keep it at a comfortable temperature. I hook my thumbs in my backpack straps

8

and quicken my pace, my dorm building coming into sight.

If it wasn't for my grumbling stomach, I might have tried holding out for a bit longer to get The Chair. But I doubt the victory of outlasting him would have been as sweet with my insides aching from hunger.

I'll just have to try again tomorrow. On Wednesdays, I can usually beat him there. Tuesdays and Thursdays, he seems to have a leg up. His professor probably lets him out early.

That's never the case with mine. When I was accepted into the chemical engineering program, I knew it would be tough, but this is another level. My professors don't waste a minute of their classes when they can use that time to stuff more equations and theories into my poor, overworked brain.

Lucifer is probably taking some filler elective, which he skips half the time just so he can get to The Chair before me.

Bastard.

Giggling mixed with deep laughter drifts through the thick metal door to my dorm suite, and it's all I can do not to let out a groan.

Hasn't my afternoon been filled with enough annoying people? What did I do to piss off the universe today?

When I push the door open, the exact scene I was expecting greets me—my roommate, Alexis, sprawled on the couch with her boyfriend, Mitchell. They aren't doing anything inappropriate, like having sex in the middle of the common room. No, what makes me cringe is—

"Hey, Hannah! Whoa, look at that backpack. It's as big as you! Why do you need so many books? I thought you were just born, knowing all that shit. Didn't your parents teach you calculus when you were, like, five?" Mitchell laughs at his own joke, and Alexis snorts along with him.

"Yeah, no. I've got to study like everyone else." My answer comes out flat, and I don't linger.

Even though I power past them, his voice still follows me down the hall to the bedroom I share with his girlfriend.

"Yeah, right. Bet when you walk in the class, the professor takes one look at you and is like, *Okay, automatic A!*"

After close to two semesters of Mitchell's jokes, I thought I might be used to them.

But no. Each one still makes my skin itch like his words are pepper spray. And they never stop. Pretty sure the only thing the guy sees is that I'm Asian. Like I'm not even a real person to him.

One time, I tried talking to Alexis about it.

It didn't go well.

"He's just making jokes! And he's calling you smart! It's a compliment more than anything."

Yeah, right. I'd like to watch her repeatedly get boiled down to one stereotype and then ask if she sees it as a compliment.

Maybe I'd do better with it if he wasn't around all the time. Our freshman year, Alexis and I were pretty close. We'd stay up late, watching TV and eating crappy food, complain about our professors, and gossip about the cute boys who lived on the floor below us. Then, at the end of the year, Alexis started dating one of those boys, and the tentative friendship we'd started to build got put on hold.

I hoped to find her on her own tonight, so I could ask if she wanted to come to the dining hall with me. But no way can I put up with Mitchell for an entire meal.

My bed gives a groaning squeak when I toss my backpack onto it, and I snatch up the newest fantasy novel my sister mailed me.

She's always sending me books after she finishes them, expecting me to text her my thoughts when I'm done. Good thing we both like kick-ass heroines battling vampires, werewolves, trolls, and all manners of other mythical creatures. The spine is creased beyond recognition, so this must be a good one.

Knowing that I'll get lost in the pages is the only solace I have as I slip out of the dorm to head to the dining hall, alone.

Again.

3

NATHAN

How is it already Wednesday?

I shouldn't have put this off so long.

My bag sits heavier because of the weight of my deadline, the strap cutting into my shoulder. Two days until not only a detailed lesson plan is due, but also a write-up on the theory behind my activity choice.

Whoever thought getting a degree to teach elementary school kids was easy was vastly mistaken.

Can't I just hang out with kids all day, making fun crafts and playing ridiculous games?

Apparently not. Shaping young minds is not something the university takes lightly. They expect me to work my ass off for the chance.

But I know I can get the assignment done. I just need to buckle down and concentrate.

No luck of that if I head back to my dorm.

There's only one place I know where I can get a few solid hours of uninterrupted work time.

The library lobby is teeming with people, and I maneuver around them to reach the elevator. The Spot won't have loud, chattering crowds. Up there, I'll be able to sink into the cushy chair and concentrate on my notes.

Or at least, I'd be able to if Shorty wasn't already there. Her midnight waterfall of hair obscures her face as she bends over a textbook and scribbles a furious stream of notes.

A sigh leaks out of me. I accept temporary defeat and trudge over to the desk she resigned herself to yesterday when I was the victorious one. It's a sad replacement for The Spot, but maybe she won't be long.

As if hearing my thoughts, Shorty glances up at me, tucking her hair behind her ear in the process.

She's got on another one of her funky outfits. High-waisted turquoise shorts and a crop top with text printed on it. I wish I could get close enough to read the words.

Immediately after meeting my eyes, she shifts them away, pretending the gaze-clashing meant nothing. But there's no hiding the triumphant smirk curling her lips.

A muffled snort escapes me as I drop my bag next to the third-rate chair I'm left with. As I pull out my laptop, I let my stare wander back to her.

She sets her notes aside, and I pause in my unpacking to see if she's about to head out, leaving me with The Spot. But my hopes are quickly squashed.

Instead of putting her things away, Shorty reaches into her backpack to pull out more items. A textbook, a folder, another textbook. And from beside the chair, where I couldn't see at first, she lifts up a lunchbox and starts to unload a sandwich and bag of chips. Each item gets placed on the coffee table in front of her with deliberate precision.

And the message is clear.

Fuck off. The Spot is mine.

I turn my head away, so she won't see the ridiculous grin

spreading across my face. For some reason, I find her silent statement hilarious.

And I look forward to the next time I have the upper hand.

4

HANNAH

He'd better not be doing what I think he's doing.

It's Thursday afternoon, and to my unfortunate lack of surprise, Lucifer has beaten me to The Chair again. With the dwindling light outside the window, it would be nice to have a lamp just over my shoulder instead of relying on the fluorescent lighting high up above me.

A luxury my nemesis is not taking advantage of.

Because he's sleeping.

The guy has his feet propped up on the table again, fully reclining in The Chair, with his head tilted back. At first, I thought he might just be giving his eyes a break from the textbook in his lap.

But the slack jaw letting out faint snores is undeniable.

Hot fury pounds at my temples at the sight of my precious chair being used as this asshole's makeshift bed. He passed out and is therefore unable to appreciate the fact that he has the best seat in this building.

I can't just let this go. I'll implode with self-righteous anger if I have to sit here, watching him take advantage of The Chair.

Fists clenched, I shove up from my seat, abandoning my Organic Chemistry notes, and march the few steps it takes to end up beside him.

Yep, there's no doubt.

Lucifer is definitely asleep.

Using the end of my pen, I jab him in the arm. In his sleep, he frowns, but then he just turns his head to the side, his eyes remaining closed.

Bastard.

My poking method proving unsuccessful, instead, I grab his shoulder and give it a shake before stepping away from him. Some people wake up dramatically, and I don't want to get hit.

I shouldn't have worried though. Lucifer takes his time in shrugging off sleep, slowly blinking the haziness out of his eyes as they wander around, eventually landing on me.

"Hmm, what?"

"You were sleeping." I hope the curt edge in my voice will help cut through some of that dopey tiredness on his face. This guy needs to be fully conscious for me to properly chastise him.

"Oh. Okay."

Not even a smidgen of remorse. And Lucifer doesn't go back to reading his notes or decide to get up and vacate The Chair to someone who actually wants to use the seat for its intended purpose.

Instead, he just stares at me.

"No. It's not 'okay.' " I use air quotes to emphasize the stupid word he mumbled. "If you want to sleep, go back to your dorm. The library is for studying. You can't just claim the comfiest chair in the building and pass out in it."

His answer comes with a slow smile that somehow makes me angrier. "And you're what, library security? Here to kick me out?"

My breath comes out in a big, hot, angry huff, like a fire-breathing dragon.

"Don't get snarky with me."

"Wouldn't dream of it, Shorty."

For a moment, words leave me, and I'm left gaping at the asshole in silence. Then, the power of speech restores itself in a searing rush, and I straighten up to my five-foot-one stature, fists on my hips as I glare down at him.

"Height is a genetic feature that can't be controlled and is a pointless thing to mock." With rage smoldering in my eyes, I let my next words growl from my throat. "Being a dick, on the other hand, is a choice."

During my tirade, the guy watches me, his smile widening to a grin.

I ignore it and finish my declaration. "*You* are a dick."

Before Lucifer can respond, I storm back to my table and sit down. Hard. Briefly, I consider leaving altogether, but I won't let Lucifer drive me out of the library. I have just as much of a right to be here as he does, and I won't let petty insults intimidate me.

A few minutes pass in tense silence, and I resolutely don't look over at The Chair or its undeserving occupant.

"I'm Nathan." The guy's smooth voice fills the quiet in this back corner of the library, and I'm surprised enough to glance up at him. He's leaning forward in his seat, elbows resting on his knees, searching eyes focused on me. "And you are?"

My name sits just behind my lips, manners pushing me to give it to him.

But he already has *everything*.

Through my annoyance, I can still see how attractive his face is. Not in the *chiseled male model* kind of way. More like the *I can be hot, but I can also be goofy* way. And his T-shirt molds over a nicely toned body, lean and muscular, like a swimmer.

So, he's good-looking, and he has The Chair.

But he doesn't get my name.

With determined nonchalance, I return to my notetaking and answer in a dismissive voice, "I'm Shorty, apparently."

When his light chuckle drifts across the quiet space, I ignore the goose bumps it raises on my arms.

5

HANNAH

I BARELY DARED TO HOPE, but when I turn the corner, The Chair
sits empty.

Glorious day!

My feet kick up in a happy skip as I cross the rest of the way,
only to stutter to a stop when I realize there is actually something sitting in my seat. Only it's a sign rather than an annoy-
ingly cocky boy.

In red letters, the word *Reserved* shouts out at me from the
tented piece of paper. Underneath the bold proclamation,
there's some smaller type. I snatch up the sign to read whatever
the explanation is.

*This spot is reserved for Nathan Cooper, a very smart, very hard-
working elementary education major. If anyone—especially the
notorious spot-stealer known by the name of Shorty—attempts to sit
in this chair, they will promptly have the library police called on
them. You have been warned.*

. . .

As I make my way through the note, my mouth pops open in outrage. Then, when I'm just about to crumble the offending piece of paper up, a heavy presence fills the air on my left. Before I register my mistake, Lucifer lands with a bounce on The Chair, which I didn't sit down in while reading.

"Hey, Shorty. Glad you saw the sign." He gazes up at me with a self-satisfied grin.

I want to punch him right in the junk.

"No." Like I was planning before, I ball up the paper and spike it at his forehead.

He dodges, chuckling all the while.

My blood boils up to my face. I'm sure it's splotching up nicely. "I was here first. Get your ass out of that chair."

One of his eyebrows arches slowly, and he crosses his arms, still smiling like a doofus. "Or what?"

"Or"—my breath fills up my chest, as if puffing it out will somehow make my short stature more intimidating—"I'll make you."

Shit, that was not a good threat at all, which is obvious by the smirking shake of Lucifer's head.

FYI, I refuse to use his real name before I get any sort of proof that he is not in fact the devil.

"I need details, Shorty. How will you make me?"

The question is a reasonable one. He's probably got a good sixty pounds and ten inches on me. A physical altercation would really only work if he was a gentleman about it and let me push him around.

No way can I trust my nemesis to be a gentleman.

There's no actual library police despite what his ridiculous note said, and running to the front-desk workers feels too much like tattling in a preschool class.

Though it stings, I realize that today is another battle I'll have to lose. But that's only so I can fight again another day. And next time, I'll be utilizing guerrilla tactics.

"I wasn't finished." I cross my own arms and glare down at him. "I'll make you *pay*." The effort I put into adding a sense of foreboding to my words is wasted, as he just snorts.

"And how do you plan on doing that?"

Concluding that my angry eyes aren't doing anything to intimidate him, I flip to the other end of the spectrum and try my best evil smile as I wag a finger in his face.

"Nuh-uh. That's not how this works. Give up the seat, or face the consequences. This is your last chance."

If anything, he appears happier. "I choose door number two. Make me pay, Shorty. Do your worst." He braces himself with a cheerful grin, as if he thinks my sneak attack will come right now. When he's ready for it.

Amateur.

"Don't worry." I turn on my heel, heading back toward the stairs and praying that Alexis and Mitchell found somewhere other than the dorm to hang out. "I will."

6

NATHAN

MY FINGERS TAP impatiently on my leg as the elevator crawls upward. Shorty always beats me on Wednesdays, so I know she'll be sitting there when I turn the corner. Maybe she'll glance up from her notes and give me one of those searing glares she's perfected. They definitely burn, but I doubt it's in the way she's hoping they will.

And if she's in The Spot, then she'll stick around. Not like yesterday. Maybe it was stupid to goad her with that sign. If anyone had seen me put it there before I hid behind a bookshelf to wait for her, they would've thought I was as mature as the elementary school kids I want to teach.

But her reaction was worth it. All up until she walked out.

I hadn't wanted her to leave.

But today, she'll stick around. Today, I'll be able to pretend like I'm the one put out. Maybe she'll even take her revenge—whatever that entails. Growing up with a brother I regularly got into fistfights with, I'm pretty sure I can handle whatever Shorty throws at me.

And maybe I'll finally find out what her real name is.

The elevator bell dings, and I suppress my grin, trying to keep a neutral face. But my effort is pointless.

The Spot is empty.

I peer around, as if Shorty will spring out from somewhere, maybe with a water balloon aimed at my head. That would be priceless. But the floor is quiet.

Slowly, cautious as a gazelle approaching a watering hole, I walk toward the chair. I even go so far as to slide my bag off my shoulder and sit down, all the while braced for a sneak attack.

Nothing comes.

I beat her to The Spot on a Wednesday. What should've felt like a triumph actually bums me out.

What if she shows up and then turns back around to leave again?

I consider moving over to the uncomfortable wooden chair, but I don't want to give up our game yet. The *no longer silent* war is my connection to her.

Instead, I stand up and head for the stairs. Going up one floor, I wander around the stacks, killing time.

Giving her a chance.

After twenty minutes, I figure even if whatever class she was in ran long, she should be in The Spot by now. Excitement thrumming through my veins again, I jog down the stairs and burst through the door, figuring she'll like it if it looks like I was rushing, attempting beat her here.

But all the eagerness drains out of me when I turn the corner.

Still no Shorty.

Giving up the pretense of letting her win, I settle into the lounge chair. I only take one book out of my bag, hoping that if it appears like I might leave at any minute, she'll decide to stick it out when she eventually shows up.

Problem is, she never does.

I stay for three hours, one more than I normally do, and no sign of her. Disappointment spears through me when I accept that she's a no-show and load my textbook back into my bag.

Tomorrow, I'll slowly walk over from my class. Maybe she'll beat me, and we can have our next battle then.

But Thursday comes, and when I get to The Spot, it's empty again. Hours go by with me sitting on my own. Every slight sound has my head whipping toward the corner, waiting for her to jog around it, scowling at me and revving for a fight.

Again, she never makes an appearance.

Friday nights, I tend to meet up with some friends and go out to a bar or maybe scan a dating app to see if anyone piques my interest and is up for a last-minute date. For some reason, this Friday, I'm walking through the library's doors because one time, a few months ago, I thought I might have seen Shorty headed here on a Friday evening.

Even though I didn't let my hopes get too high, they still take a plummet when The Spot is empty for a third day in a row.

As I head back out into the cool night, I realize that other than winter and spring break, this is the longest I've gone without seeing Shorty since the beginning of my junior year. And for some odd reason, that worries me.

Did something happen to her? Is she sick?

I don't even know her real name, so it's not like I can ask around.

Pulling out my phone, I text some buddies about meeting up. All the while, in the back of my mind, an annoying thought scratches at me.

If this is how she's making me pay, it's too high a cost.

7

———

HANNAH

WEARING shorts today is pushing it. The clouds are out in full force, meaning the air doesn't have the nice warmth it's been teasing me with the past few weeks. But I just got back from visiting my family in New York and after dealing with Rochester cold, the idea of putting on pants this morning made me want to cry. So, I compromised by tugging on a sweatshirt over my cropped tee.

Besides, with the fast pace I'm setting for myself, I'll be warm in no time. And then I'll be comfy in no time because, today, I'm getting The Chair.

I'm sure of it.

At least, I am until I glance to the side and see my nemesis on a path across the quad. Lucifer strolls along with a couple of guys, laughing at something one of them said. The large, grassy expanse separates us, but somehow, he senses my gaze and turns to lock eyes with me.

We both freeze.

His body is facing the same direction mine is—toward the

library. In a twisted act of fate, we are almost the exact same distance from our destination.

As we reach this conclusion at the same moment, it's like a starting gun fires off for only the two of us to hear.

Screw power-walking.

I sprint.

As if this were meant to be an obstacle course rather than a straightforward race, there's suddenly an insane amount of people to dodge around. I dart and sidestep the pedestrians until I come upon the mammoth of hurdles—a pack of sorority girls.

"Move!"

They gasp and glare at me as I bolt through the gaggle of them. Good thing I'm not planning on pledging.

I track Lucifer out of the corner of my eye. He's running just as fast as me, his friends abandoned, his bag slapping against his leg as he sprints. Instead of following the curving paved path, I make myself a shortcut by vaulting over a bench. My landing is marred by a brief stumble that I quickly recover from, but it's enough to give him the advantage.

Ten feet in front of me, he whips open the glass doors and disappears inside.

Some people might give up at this point. But the race isn't won until there's a butt in The Chair.

When I slide through the front door, a crow of triumph wrenches out of my throat at the sight of him waiting at the elevator.

Lucifer's jaw goes slack as I blaze past him, my eyes on the entrance to the stairs. His heavy footsteps pound behind me, the short lead I gained disappearing.

In the stairwell, our panting breaths echo off the cement walls. I use the railing to pull myself up the steps faster, but there's something to be said about having a few extra inches on each leg. My competition is able to mount two steps at a time, quickly catching up to me.

I throw out an arm, as if I could stop him, but he tosses a grin over his shoulder as he easily brushes past me.

Damn him.

We're at the third-floor landing, and he's two steps in front of me, reaching for the door, pausing for less than half a second to swing it open. My frustration pours a last bit of turbo fuel into my muscles, and in a desperate move, I crouch before launching myself at my nemesis.

If he were wearing a backpack like me, I would probably slide off. But this pompous ass went for a shoulder bag, so I have free rein to latch onto him.

"Wha—"

His question is cut off by my vise grip on his neck, and committing fully to the move, I sling my legs around his waist.

"Can't sit down if you don't have a back!" My proclamation won't win any Academy Awards, but I'm pretty pleased with it.

Lucifer wraps his large hand around my wrist, and I fully expect him to pry me off. Instead, he merely tugs my arm down enough to release the pressure on his throat. Then, surprising the hell out of me, he moves his other hand to cup my thigh.

It's almost as if he's supporting my weight. Like we're friends and he's giving me a piggyback ride.

Like this isn't a battle of epic proportions.

As we wobble drunkenly, locked together, I try to come to terms with his warm palm on my exposed skin. Then, I get another shock when the expanse of his back, pressed tightly against my front, begins to shake.

With all the adrenaline coursing through my body, I take longer than I should to realize that he's cracking up.

"You-you climbed me! Like I'm a-a tree! An-and you're a sq-squirrel!" he chokes out the comparison and actually falls down to one knee because he's laughing so hard.

This is my chance. I should let go, push him to the side while he's distracted. Claim my prize.

But I can't seem to convince my arms to release him. Instead, I hold tight, committing to wherever this wild ride takes me. I'm entwined with a virtual stranger, yet for some reason, the embrace doesn't seem awkward at all.

With my head practically buried in his neck, I can't help breathing in whatever that amazing soap is he uses. Lucifer belongs in a spice rack, the smell of cloves clinging to his messy brown hair.

Unaware that I've upped my crazy factor a few more notches by sniffing him, he gasps out a couple more chuckles before standing up again. Wearing me like a jacket, he saunters through the shelves.

"Don't know how you expect this to work, Shorty."

He turns his head to smile over his shoulder, and I rear mine back, so I can properly glare at him.

"I expect you to admit that you've been physically bested and to give up The Chair."

"Oh, physically bested, am I? Well, from my angle—"

My gasp cuts off whatever witty comeback he might have had.

Lucifer whips his head around, and no doubt, he immediately sees what brought on my horrified reaction.

The sight is so devastating that I lose all strength in my limbs, sliding down his body to settle unsteadily on my feet.

"The Chair ..." I whimper.

The humor has disappeared from his face. All that's left is angry bewilderment.

"It's gone."

8

NATHAN

SHORTY STOMPS out of the elevator. The angry walk makes her round bottom bounce.

She'd probably punch me in the stomach if I pointed it out. And even worse, she'd probably try to make it stop.

I can't believe she jumped on me.

The sensation of her clinging to my back isn't something I'll soon forget. She was all muscular legs and hot breath on my neck. When I got over how hilarious it was, my body picked up on the fact that a cute girl was wrapped around me. And now, I'm having trouble focusing on anything other than how I can convince her to climb up on me again.

Even my irritation about someone ruining The Spot is hard to hold on to as I trail after her fuming little form.

Then, I remember that The Spot is all that ties us together. Without it, she might dismiss me from her day-to-day life.

Can't have that.

"Excuse me." Shorty raps her knuckles on the front desk to get the student worker's attention.

The tall blonde girl turns with a smile that falters. Having been on the wrong end of Shorty's glares before, I have an idea of what she's seeing.

Pure intimidation.

"How can I help you?"

"There's a leather armchair that is normally on the third floor by the side window. It's gone. Where is it?"

A few passing students slow down like rubberneckers on the opposite side of the highway from a car crash. Drama is a teasing scent in the air.

"Oh, um ... I-I think someone moved it."

"Moved it?" Shorty's question growls out of her throat.

I bite my lip to keep from grinning and prepare myself to grab her if she decides to launch herself over the desk at the innocent library worker.

"Yeah, I think so." The girl fiddles with her hair as her eyes dart from side to side.

"Where exactly did they *move* it?" Shorty spits out the word *move* as if it had a nasty taste.

The worker swallows before speaking, "Um, I might have seen it in the basement. Maybe."

"The basement!" My competitor throws her hands up and finally leaves the poor girl alone, plowing through the curious onlookers without acknowledging their existence.

I jog after her as she stalks back toward the elevator.

"Probably some full-of-themselves upperclassmen moved it. Think they run the place."

"Yeah. Bunch of assholes. Am I right?" I nudge her with my elbow as we wait. The gesture earns me a glare.

"I'm not fully convinced this isn't your doing." She runs her eyes over me, frowning all the while.

Instead of being intimidated or offended, I bask in her scrutiny. Shorty is back and in full force. She had me worried last week, but when I spotted her this morning, a surprising rush of excitement filled my chest.

The doors slide open, and she takes her gaze away from me when she moves forward. Like a besotted puppy, I follow right on her heels.

"I might mess with you, Shorty, but I'd never desecrate The Spot." My fingers catch a lock of her hair, and I give it a playful tweak.

The scowl she hits me with this time appears softer. As she bats my hand away, I catch a slight twitch at the corner of her mouth.

"Not sure I can trust you, Lucy."

"Lucy?"

There's a clear twinkle in her eye this time when she looks up at me. "Short for Lucifer."

I choke out a disbelieving laugh as she fights a grin.

"Where'd that nickname come from?"

Instead of answering, she tightens her lips and stares at the doors.

"Let me guess … it's because I'm devilishly handsome, isn't it?" I make my best effort to waggle my eyebrows.

She snorts and gives me a shove just as the elevator opens up to the basement.

Before I can regain my balance, Shorty sprints out the door. That little head start is all she needs.

"Aha!" Sitting by a cluster of couches is the missing chair. Without any preamble, she belly-flops onto it. "I win! It's mine!"

I follow at a more sedate pace, watching her wriggle around on the seat, wearing a huge grin. The sight has me struggling to clear my throat. I thought she was cute when she was angry with me, but this happy, beaming version of Shorty puts all others to shame.

Maybe I should spend more of my time trying to get her to smile rather than scowl.

Too bad I have to point out an unpleasant reality.

"Not sure this is over quite yet, Shorty."

She pops up, sitting cross-legged in the chair, her face falling back into a defensive frown. "Yeah, it is. I'm here. I've got the chair. Accept your defeat."

I snort before crouching down beside her. "You're really going to tell me the chair is all you care about? That it's the only thing that makes The Spot so great?"

Her eyes won't meet mine as she pinches the leather on one of the armrests.

I push a little more. "You're fine with sitting down here? In the basement? No windows? No nice lamp? No coffee table?"

She groans and collapses back on the chair, her backpack making her spine bow out at a dramatic angle. With her sitting like this, her chest presses against the baggy material of her sweatshirt. I can make out the slopes of her breasts, reminding me of the pleasure of having them molded against my back just a few minutes ago.

"Okay." Her answer pulls me back to the present. "You're right. It's not just the chair."

She struggles to lift herself up, so I stand with an extended hand. After a side-eye look at it, she concedes and slides her palm into mine.

The touch of her soft skin against mine is too good to give up. When she's on her feet, I keep ahold of her as we stare down at the chair.

"This is a two-person job. I think we might need to call a temporary truce."

I watch her chew on her lip as she glances between the piece of coveted furniture and the elevator. "What are the terms of the truce?"

Her hand is still in mine, which I take as a positive sign.

"Terms ... good idea." I fiddle with her palm as I sort through different options, fascinated with the small calluses I find at the base of a few of her fingers. "How about we work together to put the chair back, and then we flip a coin? Winner gets The Spot today."

When I look down to see how she takes my suggestion, I find her watching our hands. I bite down on my lip to keep from smiling.

"Okay. I can agree to that."

Success.

Time to give another push. "And you tell me your name. Your real name."

That gets her peeking up at me, a self-satisfied smirk decorating her round face. Maybe I shouldn't have shown my hand. Now, she knows she has something I want. And if I thought she'd give that bit up without anything in return, I was naive.

"That's not really balanced, is it? I should get something else too."

"Oh, really? Like what?"

She purses her lips and squints her slim eyes as she stares at me. Then, like the sun bursting from behind a cloud, a glorious grin spreads across her face.

"You have to tell me an embarrassing story about yourself."

Sneaky little witch.

"You think that's a fair trade?"

She shrugs. "You tell me. What's my name worth?"

This girl might actually be a witch, come to think of it. I've just noticed the design on her sweatshirt, some kind of satanic symbol—a pentagram inside a sun-shaped circle.

Maybe she cast a spell on me, and that's why I'm happy to spill all my secrets to her.

"Okay, Shorty," I sigh. "A name for a story. But you'd better pull your fair share when it comes to moving this thing."

"Yeah, yeah. Let's just see if you can keep up." She's the one to drop my hand first.

I'm not sure I would've let go otherwise, which would've

made the next ten minutes even more of a struggle. Between the two of us, we heave the armchair across the lower level and then tilt it at an awkward angle to fit it in the elevator. Shorty ends up wedged against the back corner, completely blocked in by the piece of furniture. I squeeze myself in and press the third-floor button.

"You know, if I was really cruel, I'd leave you in here." Standing up straight and tilting my head to the left, I can just make out her glaring eyes.

"Try it. See what happens."

My chuckle fills the tight space as we inch between floors, and then I give in to my curiosity. "What's that symbol on your sweatshirt? You worship Satan? But wait ... wouldn't that mean you worship me?" I let my wicked thoughts spill into my grin.

She rolls her eyes. "You are the devil; that's for sure. And it's from a TV show. Which, FYI, you just lost major points for not knowing."

"What show?"

But she just shakes her head, leaving me kicking my past self for not consuming every aspect of pop culture in order to impress sassy girls I meet in the library.

When the door pops open, there's some more creative maneuvering and a decent amount of cursing on both our parts before we're able to exit the elevator. But after that, it's smooth sailing with Shorty doing a surprisingly good job at holding up her end of the chair. She's hiding some power in that tiny body of hers and showing it off in all sorts of impressive ways today.

We stand next to each other, recovering our breath and admiring The Spot put back to rights.

"Okay. Story, then coin flip, and then name." She stares up at me expectantly.

"Story, then name, and then coin flip," I counter.

The corner of her lips quirks, and she gives me a go-ahead nod.

"Okay. I thought of one on the ride up. You ready for this?" I wait for her dark chocolate eyes to be focused solely on me. If I'm going to make a fool of myself, I want every bit of her attention. "Last summer, during a family trip to the beach, I pissed off my brother. It's a common occurrence, so I didn't really think about it. But when I fell asleep, lying out in the sun, he decided to use some sunscreen to write a little message on my back."

Shorty's teeth pinch her bottom lip as a grin threatens to split her face open. Close to a year later, I can see the humor in the prank, but at the time, I wanted to put him in a choke hold until he passed out.

"What did he write?"

I give her a good-natured grimace. "Took me a while to realize why everyone was congratulating me and telling me I looked good. The little shit had decided to borrow a line from my mom's favorite musical."

She's hooked, listening to my humiliation with wide, excited eyes.

"For the rest of the summer, I had to wear a shirt or show off the message *I Feel Pretty* to anyone who could see my back."

Her delighted gasp has me smirking in response. She stares at me like I'm free dessert.

"I think I'm in love with your brother."

The breathy statement sends a streak of jealousy shooting through me. A scowl threatens, but I try to smooth it. She's obviously joking.

"Yeah, well, he's underage. So, you're stuck with me."

She grins and leans to the side, as if to peer behind me. "It's not still there, is it?" The hope in her voice brings my smile back.

I shake my head. "Sorry, Shorty."

"Hannah."

It takes me a second to realize that she's giving me my end of the bargain.

"That's your name?"

She nods.

"Hannah," I sigh out, looking forward to saying it in all different sorts of circumstances.

"Yep. Now, flip that coin!" She rummages in the pockets of her navy-blue shorts, coming up with nothing. "You do have one, right? 'Cause I'm all out."

Hesitantly, I pull a quarter from my back pocket. I fiddle with it for a moment as if I were having trouble gripping it, stretching out the time I have with her.

But all good things must come to an end.

"Call it." With a flick of my thumb, the silver sails into the air, rotating fast.

"Tails!"

The coin lands neatly in my palm, and I slap it down fast on the back of my opposite hand. Drawing out the suspense, I peek under to catch the first glimpse.

George Washington's head comes into view, and my eyes flick between him and the eager girl in front of me.

"You're in luck." I slide the coin back into my pocket. "The Spot is yours."

The resulting happy dance is a joy to watch.

Hannah pumps her fists in the air and sways her hips back and forth, chanting, "I win! I win!" in time with her movements.

With a dramatic flourish, she drops her fat book bag onto the coffee table before turning back to me with a triumphant chuckle. "I'd say good luck next time, except ..." She trails off, the smile fading from her face as she stares over my shoulder. "Shit sticks. Really?"

I glance behind me, intending to fight whoever took away her happiness. But the space is empty. Just a few shelves and a wall with a clock.

"I can't believe this. The one Tuesday I get the chair, and my time runs out."

When I turn back around, Shorty has the straps of her bags over her shoulders.

She's leaving.

"Hey. What's all this?"

I want to step in front of her, stop her from walking away, but I hold myself back.

She grimaces. "Group project. Gotta meet my partners in the science building. Looks like you win today, Lucifer."

Hannah grins at my frown, probably thinking I dislike the nickname instead of the fact that she's about to disappear. It's not until she's almost around the corner that I get my voice back.

"Wait!"

One of her eyebrows quirks up as she pauses to look back at me.

"You didn't tell me your last name." It's lame, but it's the first thing I could think of on the fly.

Hannah shakes her head and waves, calling out to me as she vanishes around the corner, "The Chair and my first name are enough. You can't have everything!"

That sounds like a challenge.

9

———

HANNAH

THE SKY outside the window fades to twilight, but I just reach up and click on the lamp.

Perfect.

The Chair is mine tonight. Not that I had any doubt it would be. I'm one of the few students choosing to spend her Friday evening in the library.

Maybe that's lame, but at least I'm not studying.

When I stopped by the campus post office, the attendant handed me a care package from home, which included another one of my sister's selections. Starting off my weekend with a half-vampire heading up a secret government agency, tasked with hunting down rogue supernatural creatures, is as cool as it gets in my book. Literally.

The story is so engrossing that I don't even realize I'm not alone until Nathan braces a hand on the armrest at my back, so he can loom over me. His sudden appearance spurs a knee-jerk reaction in me.

Like an octopus, I throw out all my limbs. "My chair!"

His dark chuckle washes over me as he stares down at my prone form with his slumbering eyes. "I wasn't trying to steal it, Shorty."

"Why're you still calling me that?" I nudge his thigh with my sneaker. "You know my name now. Paid a high cost for it too. By the way, you look very pretty tonight."

His grimace makes me grin. I do have to admit, Nathan is slightly more handsome than is fair. Smooth, sculpted lips sit on a freshly shaved jaw. His chestnut hair seems damp, as if he walked over here after getting out of a shower.

Mmm. Nathan in a shower. Now, *that* would be pretty.

With him this close, I can pick up that subtle cloves scent. All combined, it's a little too much for me to handle.

The scowl he has on gives way to a smirk, so fast that I'm almost positive my teasing didn't actually upset him at all. "You waited too long to tell me your name. Shorty is how I think of you now."

"Well then, I'm sticking with Lucifer. I think it fits you better anyway."

In response, he reaches out to tweak the end of my braid. "Whatever makes you happy, Shorty. Now, come on. Let's get you out of the library for one night."

I shake my head, holding up my book for him to see. "I'm good right where I am."

"*One Foot in the Grave*?" he reads the title as if confused by its awesomeness. "This is your Friday night?"

"Hell yeah, it is. Vampire huntress kicking some undead ass. What's better than that?" I snatch my book away from his reaching hand.

He sighs and sits on the coffee table across from me.

I'm simultaneously grateful for the relief from his hovering and regretful that I can't smell him anymore.

"Okay, that does sound sort of intriguing. But come on,

Shorty. You can read anytime. And the library is closing in an hour anyway."

He has a point. But counterpoint, I'm very comfortable.

Clearly realizing his reasoning hasn't moved me, Nathan props his elbows on his knees before leaning toward me and throwing out probably the best offer he could make.

"You come hang out with me, and the next time I get the spot before you do, I'll forfeit it whenever you get here."

"Deal!" Maybe it would've been more prudent for me to take a moment to think his offer over, but then he'd have had the opportunity to take it back. "So, what are we doing?"

He shrugs. "Something fun."

With a groan, I slide deeper into The Chair. "It's not a party, is it? Because college parties are *not* fun. They're all over-crowded, sweaty, and full of people trying to hook up with each other." I'm whining, I know, but if I gave up a night of reading to go stuff myself in some upperclassman's crappy off-campus house, I'd be pissed.

Nathan grins and pats my knee. "Don't worry. I won't make you go to a party. We'll do something that's actually fun. But you need to come with me to find out what it is."

With that cryptic invite, Lucifer clasps my forearm to lever me out of the chair.

Once standing, I stiffen for a second, watching him with a wary eye.

"What?" He tilts up one eyebrow at my obvious tensing.

"Just waiting to see if this was all a ploy to get me out of The Chair, so you could steal it."

Instead of lunging for the soft cushions, he tosses an arm around my shoulders and scoops up my bag, sliding it onto his back.

"Not tonight, Shorty. I'm taking you out."

10

NATHAN

"I'M GONNA DIE. Seriously, this is so good; I'm going to just keel over. I can't even handle it." Hannah's eyes threaten to roll back in her head as she scoops up another piece with her fork. A happy hum emanates from her throat while she chews.

"Glad to hear I'm lethal." I give her my best smirk before taking a bite of my own.

She hits me with a friendly glare. "Stop trying to take credit. When they identify my cause of death, it won't be *Nathan Cooper*. It'll be *death by pie*."

"Death by pie, provided by Nathan Cooper," I amend.

Hannah ignores me as she licks the last traces of caramel off her fork.

After getting close to her in the library, I couldn't help taking a deep inhale of her pear scent. It made my mouth water and gave me an idea of what to do once she finally agreed to abandon The Spot.

Slice 'Em Up is a local pie shop I found at the end of my freshman year, which serves a variety of flavors. One happens to be a mouthwatering pear pie with cinnamon-caramel glaze, the filling so sweet that it makes my teeth ache and a crust so buttery that it flakes off in smooth chunks. I plunge my fork in for another round of the mind-melting taste.

On the pathway to my mouth, I realize Hannah is watching me. More specifically, she's tracking my utensil. Then, I notice her plate is polished clean while I still have a good third of my piece left.

"Guess you approve of my version of *fun*, huh?"

She doesn't acknowledge my smile, eyes glued to my food. "Still haven't passed judgment. Maybe I need more convincing."

"More convincing? Or more pie?"

Hannah's gaze flicks to mine with a smile as tempting as my dessert, and I'm incapable of denying her. Carefully, I extend my fork across our small table.

Her delighted grin holds out momentarily before she opens her mouth to accept the offering. Once the pastry sits on her tongue, I retrieve my silverware, watching it slide out of her closed lips. A flutter of her lashes and the slow movement of her jaw betray how she's savoring my gift.

Suddenly, I'm hit with the knowledge that not only does she smell like pears, but if I were to dip my tongue into her mouth right now, she'd taste like them too.

"Okay, I concede. You have mastered *fun*." Her words come out garbled from the food.

I let silence descend for a moment as I watch her finish chewing and swallowing while I consume the last bit still on my plate. The night air carries a slight chill, but Hannah doesn't seem to mind, once again wearing her overly large sweatshirt with its mystery symbol.

When we're both done, I collect our trash and toss it in a bin.

"Okay, so I guess that was a decent alternative to reading in the library. Thanks for the pie." Hannah hefts her bag onto her shoulder and makes like she's going to leave.

Without thinking, I reach out to wrap my arm around her waist and pull her in toward me. Hannah's eyes go wide in surprise, staring up at me as if waiting for an explanation as to why I grabbed her.

Thinking on my feet, I throw out the first idea that comes to mind. "Let's watch a movie. At my place."

Hell, that sounds like such a line.

"That sounds like a line." She seems to read my thoughts as she glares at me.

While I do like the idea of Hannah coming back to my apartment for some adult activities, that's not what I meant at all.

"Get your mind out of the gutter, Shorty. When I say *movie*, I mean, movie. It's still early."

She glances at the time on her phone and then gives a half-hearted shrug that sends a spark of excitement through me.

"Okay. But if you pick a crappy movie, I maintain the right to walk out."

"Deal."

As we leave the shop, she steps away from my hold. No problem. I just slide my hand into hers, lacing our fingers together.

"You're a very touchy person, aren't you, Lucifer?" She holds up our clasped palms but makes no move to detach herself from me.

Not so much with other people, but with Hannah, I can't seem to stop myself. Everything about her acts as a siren's song, luring me in, tempting me to touch and caress. She'd probably shove me away if she knew how often I imagined sliding my hands past the waistband of her jaunty shorts and cupping the bare skin of her generous ass.

For now, I'll keep my cravings to myself.

"Nah, I'm just trying to make sure you don't sprint away from me. I've seen how fast you can run."

"Honestly, I didn't know I had that kind of speed in me. You saw me ninja leap over the bench, right?" She beams up at me.

We spend the rest of the walk going back and forth about our mad dash to The Spot, and by the time I unlock my front door, we're both having trouble getting words out around our laughter.

"I just"—giggle—"jumped! Can't believe"—snort—"it either!"

"You almost strangled me!" I toss my keys on the counter.

Her hand gives mine a squeeze before sliding away. The loss takes some of my laughter with it.

"Well, now, you know. Don't mess with Shorty," she murmurs with a smile while wandering around the main room of my apartment.

The suite is in one of the older buildings on campus, which people might think makes it appear quaint because it's historical. I'd like those people to try living in the place during the last few weeks of summer and see how they enjoy not having any AC. Still, despite the drafty windows and low ceiling, these suites are pretty coveted because they each have two single bedrooms, and they're some of the few places on campus that aren't dry.

As in, if you're twenty-one, feel free to stock up on alcohol.

Speaking of which ...

"You want something to drink? I've got beer."

In the past, when I brought a girl over and said the same line, the response was always excitement. Everyone is eager for a drink.

Should've known Shorty wouldn't fit in with the mold.

"I'm twenty." She lets her bag drop onto the scarred hardwood floor and examines one of my roommate's concert posters he's tacked up on the wall.

"I won't tell if you won't."

Hannah shifts her stare over to me, eyes wide and blinking. "Is ... is this what it feels like?"

My brain stutters over her reaction. She looks so lost.

"What *what* feels like?"

Just as quickly as the innocence appeared, it's gone, and her face falls into mock disappointment. "Peer pressure, of course. My parents warned me about people like you. Out to corrupt the innocent."

Back on firm ground with our joking, I affect a frat-guy tone. "Come on, Shorty. All the cool kids are doing it."

"Just what I expected, Lucifer." Her eyes smile as she sucks on her bottom lip. The sight is so distracting that I almost miss her next words. "You're gonna have one, right? I'll try some of yours."

"What is it with you tonight? Eating my pie. Drinking my beer. Soon, you're going to demand fifty percent of my assets," I call out to her while pulling a bottle from the fridge. When I pop off the cap, a light mist drifts out of the cold glass neck.

Shorty approaches, and when I hand the beer to her, she suspiciously sniffs the contents. A thought dawns on me.

"You've really never drank before?"

Only when the words are out, do I realize how condescending they sound.

"Nope. Never got the urge. Don't really have it now either, but"—she shrugs—"it's here. I'll try it." With that unenthusiastic declaration, she takes a swig.

Then, she immediately spits it out.

In my face.

"Ugh! What the—oh my God! Nathan, I'm so sorry!"

Stunned, I haven't moved. Instead, I just let the mixture of beer and spit drip from my cheeks. I don't even know what to do.

The caress of something soft and dry wiping over my face

brings me back to life, and I reach up to find Hannah grabbed a kitchen towel to clean me off.

"I swear, I didn't plan that. Only, if you're going to try to make me do something illegal, you could've at least made it taste good."

That does it. I snatch the towel out of her hand and bury my face in it. The noise I make is only slightly muffled by the fabric.

"Are you ..." She hesitates over her question. "Are you crying?"

Hannah's worried tone only makes me howl all the more. It's too much. I collapse against the wall, letting the towel fall away so she can see that I'm barely breathing from laughter.

Through my tears, I watch her eyes narrow and the corners of her mouth twitch.

"You are"—I don't think I'll be able to finish the thought as I choke on my own breath, but I force the last word out —"amazing."

That gets her full grin and a nonchalant shrug. "Well, yeah. Duh."

I have to leave the room, partly because that's the only way I'll recover from my hysterics, but also because I need to put on a clean shirt. When I come back, my breath is under control, and Hannah is sitting on the couch while she unties her sneakers.

"Okay. So, what do you actually want to drink? I think we've got some soda, and there's always water." When I grab the fridge handle, I realize she's followed me into the kitchen, her bare feet not making any noise on our creaky, old floor.

"Do you have any milk?"

"Milk? Um, yeah. Whole okay?"

Bobby, my roommate, drinks it for the protein content, apparently.

"Perfect. My mom just sent me a fresh bag of hot chocolate mix."

I expect her to be holding one of those individual Swiss Miss servings from a box. Instead, Hannah clutches a gallon-sized ziplock full of an unlabeled brown powder.

"Your mom sent you that?"

She nods while pulling open cabinets like she lives here. I realize I don't mind her heavy-handed ways.

"Need help finding something?"

"Yeah, I—never mind! Here we go." From one of the shelves, Hannah pulls down a saucepan I'm not sure Bobby or I have ever used. Probably realizing this, she rinses the thing off before placing the pan on the stovetop. Reaching over to grab the milk out of my hand, she raises a single eyebrow. "You want some too? There's plenty."

"Sure." Fascinated, I watch her bring the milk to a boil before using a spoon to scoop a generous amount of the brown powder into the pot. The mixture becomes a thick, dark chocolate color that clings to the spoon as she stirs it.

"Mugs?" Her question pulls me out of my hypnotized state.

Once everything is poured, Hannah holds hers up to her nose, drawing in a deep sniff of the cocoa. I blow on mine once before taking a sip.

"That's hot!"

She smirks. "Well, yeah, it just came off the stove."

"No, I mean, hot as in spicy. What's in this stuff?" I can't help myself from taking another deep swallow. Like anything with chocolate, the first wave I taste is a heavy sweetness, but lingering underneath the rich, expected flavor is a hint of a bite that makes my tongue tingle and beg for more.

"Mmhmm." She takes her own sip, and a smile creases her cheeks. "Cayenne. Mom adds a little bit. That's why her mix has ruined me for all store brands."

Hannah tops off both our mugs before we wander back into the main room.

Because I'm a gentleman and a good host, I give her the remote, so she can pick out the movie. I watch her as she scans through the options, my muscles relaxing as I slide down onto my secondhand couch. The two of us hanging out together comes easy, like we've been friends rather than enemies all this time.

If she disappears on me again, I'm going to have something to say about it.

"Where were you last week? I had The Spot all to myself."

"That must've been such a hollow victory for you." Her voice is laced with teasing sarcasm that has me grinning in response.

"There you go again. Assuming the worst about me. Did you consider that I might be worried about you?" I concentrate on the swirling pattern in my cocoa, trying to keep my honesty from weighing too heavy on our banter.

"You were worried? About me?"

The tone of her voice draws my eyes back to hers. An expression of complete befuddlement creases her slim brows.

Is it really so unbelievable that someone might?

"Yeah, Shorty. You disappeared on me. With no way for me to check up on you, might I add."

"But I'd only ever been mean to you."

I reach out and tweak the end of her braid. "Maybe I'm into that."

Hannah snorts. After setting down the remote, she slides her cell phone out of her back pocket and fiddles with it for a second before handing it to me.

On the tiny screen is a clear picture of two women in long, flowing dresses, as if they were about to attend a movie premiere or gala event.

"My sister's wedding. As her maid of honor, I had to be there for all pre-wedding festivities."

Because I'm dense, it takes her explanation for me to realize one of the women has on a white dress for a reason. Hannah is wearing dark purple, which contrasts nicely with her golden skin. In the picture, her hair is curled and held up high on her head. Makeup gives her face new lines and angles. She looks hot and intimidating. I prefer the more approachable version sitting next to me.

Hannah reaches over to swipe her finger along the screen, bringing up a photo with her sister and a man with one of the happiest expressions I've ever seen.

"That's Stella and my new brother-in-law, Angelo. She met him when she was studying abroad in Italy."

"Sounds like a romance novel in the making."

My comment was supposed to be a joke, but she nods emphatically.

"Oh, yeah. Most definitely. And my God, you should hear his voice. That accent is a panty-melter."

My eyes leave the phone to watch her serious face. "A panty-melter?"

"Yeah. He talks, and all the panties in the vicinity just evaporate."

I frown. "That can't be right."

She shrugs. "I think it's just the next step in evolution. But I can see why you might be intimidated."

"I'm not intimidated!" That comes out in more of a huff than I intended.

I mean, come on. The guy isn't even that impressive. What girl wants that classic tall, dark, and handsome anyway?

She pats my hand with a consolatory smile. "Of course not."

I can't let her get away with that smug look without retaliation.

Leaning in close enough to get another whiff of her subtle,

sweet pear scent, now mixing enticingly with the smell of chocolate, I put as much sex as I can into my next words. "*Il tuo sorriso è bellissimo.*"

Hannah's jaw hangs slack, and I know I've won.

"Where did that come from?" Her question comes out breathless.

Yep, I'm definitely victorious. "My grandpa and grandma came over from Italy when they were eighteen. I might have picked a few phrases up from them." The one I just spoke translates to *your smile is beautiful.*

As Hannah stares at me with a new shine in her gaze, my heart gives a quick kick, and I hide my grin with another sip of hot chocolate.

———

HANNAH

"Get out of my way, asshole!"

"I hope that's not how you normally drive. Road rage isn't healthy."

I give Nathan an elbow in his side for his comments.

"Hey! Cheater!"

Maybe so, but it worked. On the TV screen, my colorful car swerves around his, and I've got a straight shot to the finish line. Unfortunately, I don't notice the little blue shell his character has tucked in his back pocket. Seconds before I claim my victory, my car gets creamed out of nowhere, spinning into the digital grass as Nathan lets out a maniacal laugh.

"So close! I was so close!" When I shove him this time, it's friendlier, and he chuckles all the while. It's probably best not to get too worked up about video games.

My search for a movie to watch got sidetracked when I noticed a game system tucked into the corner.

He pulled it out, revealing an old Nintendo Gamecube, and glanced between the purple game system and me. "You wanna play?"

His hopeful expression sold it for me. We settled on a classic game I at least had some experience with, even as a novice gamer—Mario Kart.

"You're getting better, Shorty."

He goes to pick up his mug, only to realize it's empty. His disappointed frown makes my cheeks tingle. I notice that his beer has been sitting, untouched, for the last hour. Looks like my innocent, underage ways are the real winner tonight.

"Quit pouting. I can make another batch."

The smile spreading across his face freezes when the door slams open. A beefy guy stumbles inside with a scantily clad girl wrapped around him. They stutter to a halt when they catch sight of us.

"Hey, man! Looks like we got the same idea, huh?"

The guy, who I assume is Nathan's roommate, nods his head my way while simultaneously cupping his companion's generous butt. It's a very nice ass, all round and perky, and the girl giggles happily at the gesture, so I don't let myself get offended.

That doesn't mean I'm okay with our video games and hot chocolate ramping up into a Friday night grope-fest. When I glance back at Nathan, I try to convey this message with a *you'd better not have the same idea* brow raise.

His apologetic grimace/eye-roll combo sets me at ease.

"Hannah, this is my roommate, Bobby. Bobby, this is my friend Hannah. And who's *your* friend?" Nathan asks the last question with an evil grin.

I'm confused until I notice Bobby's eyes darting between the girl on his hip and the rest of us, a tinge of panic widening his eyes.

"Uh, yeah. Introduce yourself, babe."

This douche doesn't even know her name.

Not that she realizes. Or maybe she doesn't care.

"I'm Mary." She waves and then tugs on the loop of Bobby's jeans as she glances toward the back of the suite where the bedrooms are.

Girl knows what she wants.

"See ya, man."

The couple disappears, their exit emphasized by a door slamming.

Nathan stands up smoothly, grabbing my empty mug on the way. "Sorry about that. He didn't used to be such an asshole."

I follow him to the kitchen. "What happened? Did he get bit by a radioactive asshole spider or something?"

Nathan snorts. "Nah. He just started going to the gym more often at the end of last year. Lost some weight, gained some muscle. Girls are interested in him now, and he's living it up."

Instead of grabbing the milk from the fridge for another round of drinks, he rinses our mugs out and leaves them in the sink. The sting of disappointment is so strong that I rub my sternum. I thought we were having a fun time.

"You don't want any more?" I pluck the bag of cocoa mix off the counter, trying not to sound desperately hopeful. But I can't help it. This is the most fun I've had on a Friday night this whole year, and I'm scared that when it's over, I'll have to go back to my boring loner existence.

This past year, I've been fighting off the crushing loneliness of not having any close friends—or even casual friends—to spend my time with. All the hours Alexis and I spent together don't seem to matter to her now that she has Mitchell. My other two roommates are members of the field hockey team and only spend enough time in our dorm to shower after practice before they're off again.

Trying to branch out, I went to the first meeting of the

university's book club back in the beginning of the fall. When suggestions were asked for, I pulled out some of my favorite novels that Stella had given me.

"Vampires? Seriously? We're not in high school anymore."

After that comment—from the president of the club, no less—I officially felt unwelcome.

Then, there was the party where I couldn't find any nonalcoholic beverages to drink, and twenty minutes in, some sweaty guy decided to use my favorite sneakers as barf target practice. No one wants to have anything to do with the girl who smells like vomit.

So, my attempts at socialization were rebuffed or ended in disaster.

But I'm a strong, independent woman, I reasoned. *Who cares if I don't have a tribe of people here?*

College is a blip on the screen of my life. I'll be done in no time. When I want to talk to someone, I can FaceTime with one of my childhood best friends. That's all I need to get through the next few years.

I almost had myself convinced. But being home last week for the wedding, surrounded by relatives and hometown friends, I got a strong sense of belonging. It made me realize how depressed I'd started to become here, hours away from my loved ones with no surrogate family in sight. Even though I enjoy my classes and the Virginia weather greets me like a warm blanket, those aren't enough anymore.

I need more from the place I'm living in. I need a tribe.

But Nathan shakes his head. "Better not. You won't want—"

Whatever he's about to say gets cut off by a loud male moan that is barely muted by the wall in between us and his roommate's bedroom. When a female gasp follows right after, Nathan winces, his eyes apologetic.

Suddenly, I understand his rushed clean-up and have to press my knuckles against my lips to keep the laughter inside.

"Now, you know why I study in the library all the time." He hurries back to the main room, scooping up my bag and holding it on his shoulder while I tie the laces on my sneakers.

My fingers quiver from contained giggles, making my knots sloppy. Once we're out the door, I let the laughter flow free.

"Poor Lucifer." I pat his shoulder as the chuckles shade my falsely sympathetic words. "The sex noises too loud for you to concentrate?"

When I go to slip my fingers under the strap so I can take my bag from him, he bats my hand away.

"I've got it, Shorty. And, yes, actually. It's not easy to plan a lesson for six-year-olds when your roommate is plowing away on the other side of the wall. Surprisingly, those two things don't mix."

I give up trying to get my bag back, instead tucking my hands into my sweatshirt pouch to keep them warm in the coolness of the spring night.

"Too bad they don't get sex ed at that age. Then, it'd be perfect inspiration."

Nathan's glare has me cackling, and I can't help teasing him the rest of the walk. He takes all my good-natured ribbing with fake scowls that do little to hide the involuntary curve of his lips.

We're almost to my dorm when I have to stop, a nagging pain in my foot growing to a point that I can't ignore it anymore.

"Wait a second. There's a rock in my shoe." I hobble over to a half-wall meant to keep students off the pristine grass, hopping up to sit on it while I reach for my sneaker.

Nathan beats me there. Kneeling in front of me, he clasps my heel with one of his long-fingered hands and uses the other to untie my halfheartedly tied bow.

The gesture is intimate, and in my panic, I do what comes naturally—make a joke.

"Are you trying to Cinderella me?"

Probably my turning a fairy-tale character into a verb is what has him pausing in the act of sliding off my purple Converse.

Through his unfairly thick lashes, he stares up at me for a moment before answering, "If you mean, force you to marry me and serve as my queen if this shoe fits, then yes. Yes, I am." His playful grin sets the same hot tingles shooting through me that his mysterious Italian words did earlier.

Nathan is flirting with me.

My sister says I'm dense when it comes to recognizing it, but this time, I'm almost certain.

Why else would he invite me out on a Friday? Joke with me? Touch me?

This has to be flirting.

Right?

"Well, we both know what I'll demand as my throne if I'm to serve as queen." I give him my haughtiest look. I don't know if he finds my joking response equally as flirtatious, but it's all I've got in my arsenal, so he'll have to take it or leave it.

"Ah, yes. The coveted chair. Well, if you are my true queen, you may have whatever your heart desires." He upends my shoe, a pebble—too small to rightfully cause the amount of pain it was—tumbling free. "The moment of truth."

I can't help my eye roll, even as his antics delight me.

And of course, my shoe slides on. Perfect fit.

"Amazing! It's fate!" Nathan even goes so far as to tie my shoe for me before standing. His boyish grin is almost too adorable to handle. "You know what this means, right?"

"Uh, my car is going to turn into a pumpkin?" I move to stand up, but he leans over me, bracketing me in by bracing his hands beside my hips on the wall.

"Wrong. This means, we are betrothed." Nathan uses an official-sounding tone, getting way too into this scenario.

I have to admit, the guy commits to a joke.

"Betrothed? That's some fancy vocabulary. Are you a *Downton Abbey* fan? Big reader of historical romances?"

He slowly shakes his head, the brush of his nose against mine showing just how close he's gotten. Suddenly, the air in my lungs doesn't seem like enough, and I have to suck in a bit deeper just so I don't get light-headed.

"I know. It's intimidating. Meeting Prince Charming face-to-face." His dark eyes flicker wickedly when I snort. "But I think we need to mark this special occasion."

"Oh, really?" *When did my voice get so breathy?* I clear my throat.

His nose brushes mine again as he nods. "A royal engagement isn't official until ..." As his words trail off, I find myself swaying forward in hopes of following them to their conclusion.

"Until?"

My answer is the soft caress of his lips against mine. He's gentle, briefly pressing his warm kiss to my mouth before retreating to meet my eyes. He smiles down at me, but the joking nature of the exchange is gone, and only a question remains.

I answer back by hooking a finger in the collar of his shirt and tugging him down to me.

This time, he lingers, exploring my mouth, sending happy jitters along my spine as he massages and gently sucks my lower lip.

It's been so long since I've been kissed; I forgot how much I enjoyed it. When people talk about being drunk, this is what I always compare it to. The way sharing a breath with someone else can make my mind go hazy and my muscles turn liquid. The scent of cloves teases my nose, and a hint of cayenne still sits on his tongue when I open my mouth enough to taste him.

I trace my fingers up his neck, twining them in the silky

mess of his short hair. With that hold, I'm able to pull him closer, delighting in his smile against mine and the hot pressure of his hands on my waist as he also tries to eliminate the space between us.

A blinding light acts like an electric poker, breaking us apart. My butt hits the brick of the wall hard as I plop back down, only realizing then that Nathan started to lift me up. My make-out partner stumbles back a step, hand shielding his eyes as muttered curses drop from the lips I just got to sample.

"What's going on here?" The deep voice from behind the light holds a sense of authority, which automatically assures me I did something wrong. Only after a second of contemplation do I realize that neither one of us was breaking any kind of rules other than maybe the social norms of PDA.

"Goddamn it. Mike? Is that you? Stop shining that fucking flashlight in my face. We're not drunk."

Nathan's angry outburst has the mystery person lowering the light enough that I can make out the form of a campus safety officer. Specifically, one of the student officers who got the job because they're criminal justice majors.

"Nathan? Sorry, man." He turns to look at me. "You all right there?"

I chuckle, not too mad about the interruption. Getting drunk on a guy's kisses in public is not my norm.

How did we go from enemies to sucking face in one night?

"I'm good. Just heading home." Too quick for Nathan to protest, I snatch my bag off his shoulder and wave at the two of them. "Have a good night, Officer. Till we meet again, my liege."

In the ambient glow of the flashlight, I can see the unhappy clench of Nathan's jaw. The sight of his discomfort adds a gloating skip to my walk. As I approach the entrance of my building, I can hear him berating poor Mike.

"Seriously? This is how you repay me after getting you through our Comm class?"

"I didn't know, dude."

A stupid grin sits on my face as I swipe my key card to unlock the door.

"Shorty!" Pounding footsteps sound behind me. "I don't have your number!"

The last word is muffled by the glass between us as the door swings shut and locks automatically. Only the people who live in this dorm have key cards that can open it. A heavy knock rings through the lobby, and when I turn to glance over my shoulder, there he is, just outside, hands on hips, eyebrows sitting high on his forehead.

I smile and wave before pointing my feet toward the stairwell.

Knock. Knock. Knock.

I'm torn. Denying Nathan's demands is a hell of a lot of fun, giving me a rush of triumph and cockiness. But the sight of the dark stairwell, leading up to a room with girls who don't really care to know me and a bookshelf full of novels that have been my only friends for months, reminds me that winning isn't going to make me happy for long.

Behind me, there's someone waiting. A guy who just wants to have a way to get in touch with me again. Someone who actually wants to spend time with me.

That doesn't mean I need to let him know how much I crave his companionship.

When I turn toward the door again, I find his eyebrows are in a dramatic downward slope, and a hint of a frown is at the corner of his mouth. Then, he has the gall to lift up his hand, extend one finger, and curl it toward himself with slow deliberation.

The bastard is beckoning me.

Why do I love it so much?

Visibly dragging my feet, I make my way back to the door, hesitating just a moment before opening it to establish my power position. I push on the cold metal bar and let in the chilly night air along with his disgruntled words.

"You didn't give me your number."

"Really?"

"Really."

"And did you *want* my number?" I can't help teasing him. It's like a knee-jerk reaction that only Nathan brings on.

He stares up at the ceiling and lets out a huge sigh. For a moment, I think I've pushed our silliness too far, but when his eyes meet mine again, the devil has on a rueful smile.

"Pretty please, can I have your number, Shorty?"

11

———

NATHAN

WHEN I WALK into the coffee shop, Hannah is already at the front of the line, one person away from ordering. I'm about to join her when her eyes stray to mine. The smile that puffs her cheeks is a better boost than any kind of caffeine.

She waves me away before I can move closer. "I got this. Grab that table. Quick!"

I roll my eyes so dramatically that there's no way she can miss it, even across the room, letting her know what I think of having commands shouted at me.

"Asshole, we're gonna lose it!"

A quick glance around the shop shows that the place is pretty crowded, and there's only one free table left. I guess Shorty's always right.

"Flavored coffee of the day, cream and sugar," I call out my order, ignoring the other patrons watching our exchange with a range of amusement and annoyance.

She nods and shoos me toward the table, her panicked gaze

taking in a pair of girls walking through the door, who glance around the shop with searching expressions.

Their eyes alight on the table, but they've got no chance. I'm already halfway there, and I've got experience with fighting tougher competition than them for coveted space.

Said competition is currently laughing at something the barista said to her. In any other situation, I'd love the sight of Hannah's eyes creased in humor, white teeth flashing in an openmouthed smile. Problem is, the barista is a halfway-decent-looking guy who seems to have more than Shorty's coffee order on his mind. He actually leans an elbow on the counter to get closer to her, an answering smile forming when she goes to whisper something in his ear.

What. The. Fuck?

Is the guy her boyfriend or something?

Hannah doesn't seem the type to go around kissing dudes and then bringing them to the place where her guy works. Maybe he's just her friend.

Her gay friend, hopefully.

The dude slides two cups across the counter to her with a wink.

My stomach churns, and my head burns hot. I hate to admit it, but I'm pretty sure my sudden onset of flu-like symptoms is actually a result of jealousy.

The emotion is new, and I'm not a fan.

It's not that I haven't been attracted to girls in the past. There've been a few relationships over the years. But I guess they were all pretty casual because I never felt particularly invested. Things always ended easily enough.

That easygoing approach doesn't seem right when it comes to Hannah Mystery Last Name. When I texted her this morning about meeting up for coffee, I didn't use the word *date*, which I'm thoroughly regretting now. The idea that some other guy might try to edge me out has my muscles clenching as if willing me to cross the room to wrap a possessive arm around her shoulders.

When did I suddenly turn into an overbearing caveman?

Luckily, the rational part of my mind points out that physically removing Hannah from the presence of anyone with a penis is unhealthy and is more likely to piss her off than endear her to me.

So, I keep to my seat.

I'm rewarded for my restraint because the moment Hannah reaches my side, she plants a kiss on my forehead before setting our coffees on the table and settling across from me.

"Good job. I thought I was going to have to brawl with someone to claim this table." Her smiling eyes watch me over her lid as she takes a sip.

I mimic her movement, too dazed to do anything else.

She kissed me. The caress was nowhere near as passionate as what we had done last night, but somehow, the sweet casualness of the gesture felt more intimate. Like she might—

The coffee hits my tongue in an unexpected briny wave, like taking a swallow of the ocean. Luckily, not much made its way into my mouth because I send it spewing over the table. The napkin Hannah is holding up to shield herself catches most of what gets sprayed in her direction.

"What the hell?" The question barely makes it out through my coughing.

"That's what you get!" Her fist pumps in the air before pointing at me in triumph.

"What are you talking about?" I pop off the lid of my drink. Inside, there's just steaming water with a strong smell of salt. "Did you do this?"

"You're damn right I did, Lucifer." Hannah wears a wild grin. "Told you I'd make you pay."

It takes me a second to remember what she's referring to. Then, her promise from a few weeks ago whispers in my mind.

"Give up the seat, or face the consequences. This is your last chance."

"You dirty little sneak." I try—and fail—not to respond with my own smile. "And you call *me* the devil."

"You practically begged for it." She wiggles in her seat, having a mini victory dance.

However, if I thought Shorty was completely ruthless, that notion disappears when the flirty barista appears beside our table.

"Sorry, man. She said it was an inside joke. And it's hard to say no to Hannah."

The guy sets a cup in front of me but keeps his interested focus on my companion. There is small comfort in the fact that she only gives him a quick nod before attaching her eyes back to me.

"Thanks, Carl. I owe you one."

"I'll hold you to that." He squeezes her shoulder before making his way back to the register, throwing more than one glance behind him at the oblivious woman across from me.

"That's your actual order. I promise," she says.

I deliberately raise one eyebrow. "Oh, and I'm supposed to just trust you now?"

The giddiness in Hannah's smile dims slightly, and she grabs on to one of my hands. "You're not mad, are you?"

The shift in her expression cuts at me, and I flip my hand in hers, so I can lace our fingers together.

"Mad that you used your evil genius mind to get revenge? Never." Without checking the contents, I brace myself and take a hearty swallow of my replacement drink. Nothing but coffee washes over my tongue, and I let go of the tension in my shoulders.

Hannah hums in the back of her throat as she sips her own drink, smiling all the while.

No wonder Carl was willing to help with her mischief. How could any guy resist the intoxicating curve of her lips?

I try not to tighten my fingers possessively. "So, that barista seemed like he had no problem acting as the accomplice."

Hannah grins. "I wasn't sure he would, but I've let him borrow my Chem notes a couple of times, so I thought I might be able to work the guilt angle. Turns out, he didn't need much convincing." She shrugs and then sets a curious gaze on me. "Maybe you have more enemies than just me on this campus."

A grunt of disapproval sneaks out before I can stop it. "After last night, I wouldn't call us enemies. Besides, I don't think I'm the reason he helped you out."

Like a curious puppy, Hannah quirks her head to the side. The gesture makes me want to pull her out of her chair and onto my lap, where I can easily kiss her puckered lips.

Instead, I explain the obvious to her, "He's got it bad for you."

A crease forms between her eyebrows before she shakes her head. "That's ridiculous. He was just being friendly."

"Trust me, Shorty. This whole time, he's been looking over here at you."

Hannah wrinkles her nose, letting out a disbelieving snort. But when she turns in her seat, it's to find Carl staring our way again. She returns his half-wave before settling back to face me.

"That doesn't mean anything."

I shake my head, slowly smirking at her, which only earns me a scowl.

"He does *not* have it bad for me. I'd be lucky if he even liked me as a friend."

"What's that supposed to mean?"

Hannah fiddles with a napkin. "I'm not stupid. I know I can be a little much. To use the words of one of my classmates, I'm 'demanding' and 'abrasive' sometimes. You don't seem to mind, which is nice."

For a second, I think she's joking. But when she continues to avoid my eyes, it's clear Hannah actually believes what she's saying.

"Of course I don't mind being around you. You're funny and ruthless and awesome."

She shrugs, even as the edges of her mouth curve upward.

I take a moment to consider Hannah's obliviousness.

Does she really think people don't like her? How could she not see the clear interest that guy has for her? Is this a common thing?

What if she's never picked up on romantic signals before?

"So, last night was the first time you ever had a beer, right?" I ask aloud.

"Yeah." She watches my face, as if trying to figure out where my random question came from, while I'm searching for a way to broach the idea that just popped into my mind.

"Was that the only first you had last night?"

Hannah chews on the corner of her bottom lip. "Are you talking about Mario Kart? Because it's been a while, but I've definitely played before."

"No. That's not what I mean." I keep my eyes focused on hers, willing her to understand my question. But my staring only makes her huff out a dramatic breath.

"If you're trying to ask me something, just do it. I'm not sure I have the energy to figure out how your mind works." She presses the coffee cup to her mouth again.

My thumb traces over the thin blue veins in her wrist, and my gaze locks on the movement, as I suddenly find it hard to meet her eyes. "Was I your first kiss?"

Her snort answers me before her words do. "What? No. How inexperienced do you think I am?"

"Well, you can't seem to tell when a guy likes you, so I just wondered ..." I trail off.

Hannah rolls her eyes and shakes her head, all at once, my idiocy too much for her to handle. "Sorry to burst your bubble,

Lucifer, but I've kissed guys before. Had a boyfriend for the last few years of high school. We even"—she leans in close, whispering to me in a hushed voice—"had sex!"

Hannah sits up and dramatically glances around us, as if worried about being overheard. All clearly an act to make me feel even more ridiculous.

Which I do. But only a little bit.

Some guys get off on the idea of deflowering a virgin. They see it as a manly power thing. I've got nothing against virgins, but I find it's easier to figure out what a girl wants in bed if she's spent some time figuring it out herself.

"Sorry. I'm an idiot. You are super experienced. A master of the bedroom."

I expect her to come back with something equally silly or at least share a grin with me. Instead, the humor trickles out of Hannah's soft brown eyes, leaving her looking embarrassed. When she drinks from her cup this time, I would bet good money it's to avoid looking at me.

"Hey, Shorty? What's up?"

Instead of answering, she tries to pull her hand out of mine, but I'm not ready to let her go. When she gives up her tugging, I lift her palm to my mouth, so I can kiss the meaty part at the base of her thumb.

That earns me a twitch of her lips, but she still keeps her eyes to herself.

"Come on. Tell me."

"It's embarrassing," she mutters, barely loud enough for me to hear.

"More embarrassing than my terrible tan lines?" I make sure to affect a horrified expression.

Hannah finally looks up and actually giggles when she sees my face. The smile doesn't stick around though. Keeping her gaze on our clasped hands, she leans closer.

"I'm bad at sex."

12

———————

HANNAH

MY CHEEKS ARE GOING to set off all the fire alarms in this place. I said it out loud, and from Nathan's *slapped in the face* expression, I have no doubt that he heard me.

Holy hell, why couldn't I just stick to the jokes? There was no earthly reason for me to tell Nathan Cooper that I was bad in bed. A better route would've been to just never sleep with him.

That seems like a forgone conclusion now.

Once he collects his jaw off the floor, he'll either punch me in the shoulder like a buddy and tell me that I'll find the right guy someday or he'll make some excuse to run like I'm showing the beginning symptoms of the plague.

Good-bye, one person I've started to feel comfortable around.

Maybe Carl would be up for hanging out?

"Why do you think that?" Lucifer digs me out of my pit of self-despair with his question.

The sound of my high school boyfriend's voice echoes in my head.

"This isn't the way it's supposed to be."

"How am I supposed to know you like it?"

"You're not doing it right."

"My ex told me."

I swear every set of ears in the coffee shop is angled toward our table. Maybe that's my paranoia, but the girls sitting behind us were having a super-animated conversation just a minute ago, weren't they? The idea of everyone in the vicinity hearing my humiliation over their morning caffeine hit makes my muscles twitch in discomfort.

"What did he say?" Nathan asks.

"Can we not talk about this here?" I know my voice comes out snappier than I want it to, but he's poking at a bruise with a sharp stick while in front of an audience.

"Let's go for a walk then."

"Huh?"

But he's already up, pulling me along with him, abandoning our table to the vultures. As Nathan drags me through the exit, I catch up—at least mentally.

He wants me to talk about it. My bedroom performance. Or really, my lack thereof.

I glance around for a conveniently dug hole for me to bury my head in. Unfortunately, the university's lawns are pristine, offering no places to hide.

"Okay, Shorty, spill it. What did that fuckwad tell you, and why did you listen to him?"

"He's not a fuckwad!" Not at first.

Derrick started out as my lab partner sophomore year of high school. We would joke and pass notes while the teacher was talking. When we started dating, it was easy. And when we slept together after junior prom, I thought everything was still good.

And for a while, it was.

Until it wasn't.

"Convince me. Because right now, he sounds like a major douche bag." Nathan keeps his steps shorter, so I don't have trouble keeping up. He swings our joined hands like we're going on a pleasant jaunt around campus.

"We got along really well. We had fun together. I don't regret dating him." I can hear the defensiveness in my tone.

He ignores it, taking a casual sip of his coffee and pointedly not responding.

My sigh comes out all huffy. "I thought the sex was good. I liked it."

Most of the time, I had orgasms with Derrick, which I read online wasn't always something girls could expect.

I'm bracing for Nathan to say something. I mean, I'm talking about sex! But Lucifer just keeps up his steady stroll.

"Are we going somewhere?"

This gets him to turn his chin toward me. "If you want. But I figured we'd just walk for a bit."

Suddenly, he releases my hand, but at the exact moment I start to miss it, the heavy weight of his arm wrapping around my shoulders grounds me. Then, hot shivers trickle across my cheek and neck at the caress of his spicy breath on my ear.

"When I went on a ski trip my senior year, my brother cut out all the ass cheeks of my underwear without me knowing. The whole weekend, I had to go commando or wear ass-less boxers."

The random story hits me like a water balloon in the face.

My brain goes on the fritz, and all I can do is stare up at Nathan in openmouthed wonder.

How is it that he's able to tell such a ridiculous story in a sexy, deep voice?

A gentle smirk drifts over his lips before he leans down to press a kiss on the side of my head.

"Wh-where did that come from?" I stutter on the question, barely having regained the power of speech.

Nathan chuckles. "You seemed embarrassed. I thought I'd put us on even footing."

This guy. My heart gives a deafening kerthunk. A dangerous reaction that I can't seem to help. A boldness overcomes me, and I wrap my arm around his waist, enjoying the soft texture of his T-shirt contrasting with the solid heat of his back.

Giving him a thank-you squeeze, I smile up into his comforting gaze. "I hope you paid your brother back."

The gentle edge of his grin turns wicked, sending more pleasant shivers over my sensitive skin.

"If you mean, did I throw out all his underwear and fill his drawers with cotton granny panties? Then, yes. Yes, I did."

The urge to laugh overwhelms me, and I bury my face in Nathan's chest, letting the hilarity loose. As I gasp in breath, my lungs fill to the brim with his clove scent, and the tension in the muscles at the back of my neck relaxes.

Maybe it's only been a couple of weeks since Nathan and I have been on speaking terms, but the way he hands over these silly pieces of his past makes me feel closer to him than some people I've known for years.

When I'm breathing normal again, I turn the two of us, so we can keep walking. The movement helps, and the words start to unravel from their tight coil deep in my chest.

"We'd been sleeping together for a few months, and I thought everything was aces. Then, he asked if I'd be up for watching porn with him. He said he'd been using it to learn new moves or something. I'd never seen any before, but I was okay with trying it out." I shrug, and Nathan's fingers press into my shoulder in a reassuring massage. "So, one night, we did. Nothing crazy, just a guy and a girl going at it. It got us both ... aroused."

My confidence wavers but more because I have a sudden image of Nathan and me sitting next to each other on a couch with a porno playing.

Would he get hard like Derrick did? Would he reach for me with his lazy gaze turning into a steady smolder?

Even if he did, I know how the rest of the scene would end —with unavoidable disappointment.

"So, we had sex. I thought it was good, but afterward, he seemed annoyed. He didn't say why at first. Eventually, he did though. We watched more porn another time, and he pointed out how it was so different from what we did. How I didn't act like the women in the videos."

Nathan's hand traces over the ridge of my collarbone. When I chance a look up at him, he's facing forward, expression blank.

It won't be in a minute though.

I brace myself for the pity.

"I ... I'm quiet. In bed. The moaning and shouting and dirty talk ... that's just not natural for me. I can't even pretend. He said it was barely better than getting himself off."

The memory of the night Derrick told me still has my whole body clenching in discomfort and shame. The embarrassment. Thinking of myself as a failure. After he made the comparison, I tried harder. But when I focused too much on what I was doing wrong, I couldn't enjoy myself. Every time, I'd slip back into being quiet.

So, he broke up with me.

"You did a bad job."

Every fiber of my body flinches in offense.

If Nathan thinks I cut myself open and laid out my insecurities just so another guy could explain how flawed I was, he's signing up for a verbal beatdown.

I'm warming up my throat for some dramatic shouting when he clarifies, "If that was supposed to convince me your ex was a decent guy, then I have to tell you, mission failed. What a jackass."

The angry words I planned to throw at him never make it off my lips.

"I mean, every guy watches porn, but you'd have to be a moron to think it was real. Those women are doing a job. Sorry, but give me a real girl who actually wants to be with me over that any day." There's not a dab of pity in his voice. It almost sounds like he's pissed.

"He didn't want a porn star. He just wanted me to be more vocal." I try to put some conviction into my words, but Nathan's raised eyebrow tells me just how weak my retort sounded.

"He's an idiot."

My eyes roll of their own accord. "Come on, Lucifer. Porn or no porn, you can't tell me guys want a quiet girl in bed. They want their praises shouted! *Oh, baby, yes, just like that!*" I'm channeling my inner Meg Ryan, and a guy passing by us gives me an appreciative stare. Once he's past, I wave at his back. "See?"

When I glance up, I expect to see Nathan in reluctant agreement, maybe showing a bit of chagrin, knowing he's one of these men with their specific expectations.

Instead, a set of devilish eyes runs over my face before he leans in close to whisper against my ear, "A quiet partner means more opportunities. Airplane restrooms, tent at a campground, dark corner in a crowded bar—"

Whatever else is on his dirty list gets cut off by my hand slamming over his mouth.

Someone overhearing might have thought he offended me.

Not the case.

I had to stop him before all my clothes combusted, and I was left standing in the middle of campus, naked and panting.

Lucifer's wicked gaze rakes over me, and then a warm, wet pressure strokes my palm.

He licked me.

I tug my hand back with a gasp, and Nathan unwraps himself from me, returning to our innocent hand-holding.

But before we take another step, the bastard has to get in one last word.

"Let me know when you want me to prove you wrong."

13
____

NATHAN

Hannah won, but I can't say I'm mad about it.

The afternoon sun spills through the glass and sets a golden cast to her skin as she types rapidly on her laptop in the coveted chair. Hannah glances up when I approach, her neutral expression taking on a triumphant smirk.

"Yeah, yeah. I know." I wave away whatever taunt she's about to throw at me as I head for the rigid wooden chair across the way. Instead of settling at the desk, I pick the seat up and carry it over to sit beside her.

"Just can't keep away from me, huh?" Her smug tone and quirked lips are too adorable.

Before I sit down, I lean over, stealing a kiss from her sassy mouth.

She lets out a happy sigh that warms my chest and convinces me to linger a moment longer before retreating.

As I move back, I catch sight of her screen and the electronic form she's halfway done filling out.

"You applying for a job?"

I'm busy pulling out my textbook and notes, so it takes me a few seconds to realize Hannah hasn't answered. When I look up for the reason, I catch her chewing on the corner of her lips while she stares out the window.

"Shorty?"

She turns at the nickname, like the sound of it is a magnet drawing her to me. I'll have to remember that. Problem is, when I finally catch her eyes, there's a clear flash of guilt.

"It's not a job application. It's a college one."

"College? I thought ... aren't you a sophomore? You're not already applying to grad school, are you?"

Hannah shakes her head and tugs at a loose thread on the hem of her shorts. Her avoidance tactics are starting up an uncomfortable burn in my chest, like the time my brother snuck a handful of ghost peppers into my cheesesteak.

"No. I'm thinking of transferring. After this semester. To a school in New York."

Yep, it's just like the hot peppers. The heat starts low and innocent and then rages into full-on heartburn, making my chest ache and digestive system twist in rebellion.

"You're transferring? Why?" I rub my sternum as if the pressing of my palm will ease the phantom pain.

Hannah stares at her lap while she answers, "It's been two years, and I still don't feel like I fit here. I mean, my classes are great. But that's not really enough for me. I guess ... I'm just tired of being on my own."

"On your own?"

"I don't ... I haven't ... hell, it sounds so pathetic." Hannah presses her fingers against her closed eyelids, so I can't see her expression when she finally explains, "I can't figure out how to make connections here. In New York, I've got my family and my friends from high school who go to local colleges. Here, I've basically been alone for two years."

The words might as well be a set of blunt knives getting shoved into my stomach.

"So, what are we then?" I try to keep the betrayal out of my voice, but she still cringes in response.

"I'm sorry. I didn't mean to imply we're not friends or whatever. More maybe?" Hannah shakes her head and leans back against the chair, turning her chin to watch me. "I like hanging out with you, Nathan. I really do. But we've been on speaking terms for, what, two weeks?"

So, now, I'm *Nathan* apparently. Never thought I'd hate the sound of my real name on her lips.

"You're one person. Awesome, annoying, and a great kisser. But—and I don't mean this to sound harsh—I know how quickly something like this can burn out." She's back to fidgeting with her shorts, and I have the urge to curl those nervous fingers into mine. "I don't think I can commit to another year down here."

My lungs struggle for their next breath, as if the air is slowly being drained from the room.

I just got her, and now, she's telling me she's leaving? The strong pressure in my chest demands me to shout that she's wrong. To tell her that nothing between us will fizzle like it did with that idiot boyfriend who didn't know what he had. Explain how I've been hung up on her for the whole year and that no way will these last few weeks of the semester be enough.

I want Hannah all day, every day.

But from the firm set of her mouth and the good-bye already forming in her eyes, it's clear that we're still in too early of a stage for her to believe me.

I'm not enough to get her to stay.

The burn continues to throb and pulse in my rib cage, marking the beginnings of a hole she's going to leave in her place. I have no idea how Hannah has had such an effect on me already, but as far as I'm concerned, she's taken up permanent residence under my skin. I'm not about to let her retreat up north without a fight.

The vague outlining of a plan forms in my mind.

She needs more than me? Maybe I can get her that. Set her up to find her place here. To want to come back to Virginia in the fall.

Hannah's back to typing on her computer, the click of the keys filling the silence between us. She's probably putting the final touches on that goddamn application. A countdown has started.

But I'm not giving up.

"What are you doing Monday at three?"

14

HANNAH

"Glad to have another member! You said your name was Hannah ..." The faculty adviser holds a pen poised above her clipboard, letting my name trail off in question.

Ready for the chaos my answer is going to bring on, I tense my shoulders and shove my hands into my pockets, keeping my sights fixed solely on the woman in front of me.

"Hannah Smalls."

There's the sound of choking behind me. I ignore it.

But I can't ignore Nathan stepping right in front of me, clasping both my cheeks in his hands and staring down at me with joy equivalent to me offering to buy him a sports car for Christmas.

"Your last name is Smalls? Hannah *Smalls*?"

The pleasant heat of his skin against mine isn't enough to keep me from scowling.

"Yeah. So what?"

He moves as if to say something, but instead, his mouth just hangs open in a grin.

This gloriously happy version of him is too much. My eyes are likely to burn in their sockets from facing the overwhelming handsomeness of him. Trying to extract myself, I wrap my fingers around his wrists, ignoring how the hairs on his arms tickle my palms.

"Lucifer—"

Whatever plan I had to move away from him fizzles to nothing when he crashes into me with a kiss meant to melt my brain and set the rest of my limbs on fire. My grip on his arms becomes vital to standing, and I let him worship my mouth as I try not to lose consciousness. We might as well be embracing in the middle of an apple cider shop because all I can smell when I breathe in is his heavy scent of cloves.

The kiss ends abruptly with a quick nip of his teeth against my lower lip. I have to blink the lust from my eyes before I can focus on his giddy face again.

A heavy throat clearing just off to my right has me shoving Nathan away. Guess I surprised him because he stumbles back, laughing all the while.

"Please don't do that in front of the children." The woman who started the whole mess by asking for my full name divides a disapproving look between the two of us.

"Sorry, Professor Wesley. I'll keep all interactions G-rated from this point on."

Not as embarrassed as me, Nathan tosses an arm over my shoulders before pulling me to the van a handful of other students have already piled into. People call out hellos to him as we approach, and Nathan introduces me around.

Their friendly smiles ease some of my nerves.

After we climb into the van and I'm sandwiched between Nathan's hard leg and the window, he reaches out to tug on a strand of my hair. The playful gesture doesn't hurt. Instead, it incites a riot of tingles scattering over my scalp.

"How long did you think you could hide your full name

from me?" Nathan takes up even more of my space by laying his arm on the back of the seat behind me. He's like one of those giant Saint Bernards that tries to crawl into your lap because they think they're still the size of a puppy, and even though you start losing feeling in your legs, you don't have the heart to shove their furry ass off.

Probably why my attempt to push Lucifer back into his seat is only halfhearted.

"Stop man-spreading."

He grins and pokes my side before I slap his hand away.

"Come on, Shorty. If you'd told me your name from the start, I could've been calling you Smalls this entire time instead."

My hair gets another teasing pull.

"What a tragedy. Anyway, I only had to hold out for a few more weeks; then, I'd have been gone, and you'd have been none the wiser. But my plans were foiled!" I give him my best mock glare, only to realize the goofy grin is gone from his face.

For a brief moment, Nathan stares down at me with a frown in his heavy-lidded eyes. Then, he lets out a sigh and gives me back some of my space. He doesn't pull my hair again, and we quietly sit next to each other for the twenty-minute ride.

Pretending like I don't know what upset him would make me naive, and I'd like to think I'm smarter than that.

Nathan likes me. Possibly even as much as I like him.

So, it makes sense that he doesn't enjoy hearing about me planning on abandoning Virginia. Maybe he thinks part of the reason I'm leaving is that I don't actually have anything more than a hint of a crush on him.

Wrong.

This guy is a drug I could easily spend the rest of my life addicted to. I want to drown myself in him. If I was guaranteed continuous doses of Lucifer for the rest of my college career, I would delete all those applications I sent out and start buying books for my next semester.

Problem is, there are no definite outcomes when it comes to infatuation. I found that out with Derrick. And the flutters I felt in my chest around my high school boyfriend are nothing compared to the flock of seagulls dive-bombing my innocent heart right now as I'm pushed up against my former nemesis.

When Derrick ended things, I spent a weekend crying. Letting myself fall all the way for Nathan risks a hell of a lot more pain if he decides I'm not the one for him.

And I have no safety net here.

Friends are good for more than just curing loneliness. One of my besties, Rachel, who I've known since kindergarten, was the one who coaxed me out of my house for the first time after my heartbreak. She got me laughing and convinced me everything would turn out all right. Then, we had a bonfire and tossed in all the pictures of Derrick and me. The way good friends do.

In Virginia, I'm on my own. If I let myself fall for Nathan and he didn't catch me, there'd be no one here to help soften the landing. I'd be left a mangled heap on the hard ground.

I can't risk that.

The bus lurches over a few speed bumps before coming to a stop. Our group spills out of the van and immediately heads into the yellow brick building.

Nathan has his smile back, nudging me and bouncing on the balls of his feet.

"This is a great group of kids. One of them, Oliver, he's so cute. He keeps these little toy cars in his pockets all the time. And Jessie, she'll probably ask what your favorite color is. Don't pick something lame, like blue. She wants specifics. Think Crayola box. And then Darnel—"

The details about the toddlers are hard to grasp when I

have this new version of my nemesis to admire. His hands dance around, and his face radiates joy. Probably without noticing, he's picked up his pace, like his body can't wait to get into the school.

I have to jog to keep up. We end up being the first of our group to reach the classroom.

When Nathan told me about the Kid Kare Club he's vice president of, I thought the idea sounded sweet. College students visit a local elementary school to hang out with some of the children who have to stay late as they wait for their parents to pick them up, giving the teachers a break.

I thought he might just be looking for something to stand out on job applications, but it takes less than a minute for me to realize he's in this for more than just his résumé.

"Nathan!"

A group of the kids scramble from the floor and barrel into my companion.

"Jungle gym!" one of the little boys shouts as he grabs for my tall friend's arm.

"Okay, okay!" Nathan laughs and then flexes his biceps.

I don't understand what the douchey pose is for until the boy wearing a dinosaur shirt launches himself into the air and loops his tiny hands around Nathan's right arm, swinging and giggling. A girl latches onto his left in the same way, screaming her joy. Two more boys commandeer his legs, hugging his calves as they sit on his feet.

He is engulfed.

As Nathan struggles to take a step with his new toddler outerwear, I realize I've never seen a larger grin on his scruffy face.

And, in that moment, I reach a deeper understanding about my nemesis.

A lot of people come to college because it seems like the

next step they have to take in their life. Maybe they choose to come in undecided, or they pick a major that sounds kind of interesting, like I did with chemical engineering. Those people might grow to love their major, or perhaps they'll try out a new one until something fits.

Nathan is not one of those people.

I know without a hint of doubt that he's meant to work with kids. Somewhere in his genes, there's a strand of DNA labeled Child at Heart. If he had to spend his nine-to-five toiling in an office, all of this light and laughter radiating out of him would be crushed.

Now, I'm not saying I'm at the complete other end of the spectrum, but becoming a living piece of playground equipment is not high on my *fun times* list. Instead, I trail behind Nathan as he shuffles across the room, weighed down by four monkeys parading themselves as human children. I enjoy watching him in his element while at the same time keeping myself separate.

Not that my ghost act lasts long.

"Hey, everybody. This is my friend Hannah." Nathan finally drops his arms, and the two little climbers tumble off in a mad chorus of giggles.

"Hannah rhymes with banana!"

Through a wild mass of curly red hair, I make out a freckled face and a mouth with one tooth prominently missing.

"That's right, Chelsea." Nathan's praise makes the girl's spotty grin grow wider. He glances back at me then, his smile nowhere near as innocent as the carrottop's.

"Don't you dare, Lucy," I mutter under my breath, shorting his normal nickname to its more kid-friendly version.

Still, should've known that you can't get anything past kids.

"Lucy is a girl's name. He's not Lucy. He's Nafan." The child, who so astutely pointed out my name sounds like a yellow fruit, tries her best to correct me. Unfortunately, the lack of all the necessary incisors means her *th* comes out as an *f* sound.

"Of course. You're right. Silly me."

The two of us girls share a smile, and I'm forgiven for nick-naming her hero.

Nathan takes pity on me, probably noticing how out of my element I am.

"Why don't you read a book to whoever wants to listen? This is really just free play until the parents get here." With two children still wrapped around his ankles, Nathan can't walk me over to the bookshelf, but he places a hand on my shoulder and turns me until I catch sight of a display of colorful covers.

"I can do that," I say as I slip away to a quieter corner of the room.

The little redhead, Chelsea, follows after me. Without prompting, she pulls out a thin paperback and pushes it into my hands.

"Dat one. Please." Her curls bounce as she sits cross-legged on a rug in front of a low stool.

Guess I have my orders.

The next hour consists of me reading book after book to a group of quieter kids while Nathan pretends to be various forms of monsters, chasing the higher-energy students around the room. The other people in the club claim activities like crafts and puppet shows. All the kids are entertained, and I have never been more in awe of teachers and parents.

They do this for *hours*.

By the time we all pile back into the van, every club member wilts in exhaustion.

Everyone, except for Nathan. If anything, it's like he absorbed all the energy the kids were wearing off.

"That was fun, right? I think Chelsea liked you. And she's a hard customer. Took me three weeks to get on her good side. Before that, she'd insisted I had cooties. Now, we're cool though," he rambles, facing me, hopefulness radiating from his eyes.

The sight breaks my heart, just a little.

I know what he wanted today to be. This was his attempt at finding a place for me. Making me want to stay.

Problem is, even though Kid Kare is a great club, it's not *my* club.

I lean in close, keeping my voice low so we don't disturb the few people in our group who've been lulled to sleep by the rumble of the van. "I can see why you love it. Those kids are obsessed with you."

Nathan follows my lead, losing some of his enthusiasm. "But you didn't love it ... did you?" he asks, not a hint of annoyance in his voice, but definitely a shadow of sadness.

For a moment, I can't meet his eyes, seeing that disappointment and knowing I could easily get rid of it.

Just say you'll stay. You don't have to go.

The traitorous thoughts pound away in my skull, making me ache to give in to them.

But I can't let myself. I've known Nathan for less than a month. Staying just for him would be setting myself up for a painful fall with nothing to cushion my landing.

"It's okay, Shorty."

My fingers, which were fiddling with the edge of my shorts, get captured by his comfortingly warm grip. When I tilt my head up to check if he's serious, my mouth is claimed as sneakily as my hand was.

The swaying of the van and the fact that we're sitting inches away from eight of our peers fade from my consciousness as Nathan treasures me with soft kisses. He places them along my lower lip and then at each of the corners of my mouth.

A smoldering starts low in my belly, sweet warmth tinged with spice, just like my mom's hot chocolate. I might as well have been lowered into a bathtub full of the dark, decadent beverage. Only the delicious taste on my tongue isn't candy. It's Lucifer.

After a moment more of the chaste torture, he pulls away enough to meet my eyes.

"I'm not giving up."

15

HANNAH

"W‍HAT'S TAKING YOU SO LONG?" My voice comes out in a high-pitched whine, but I figure a guy who wants to spend all day around kids can handle a little complaining.

"Simmer down, Shorty. You want me to come out there with no pants on?"

Even with the dressing room door between us, I can still hear Nathan's voice through the wooden slats. His question brings an intriguing image to my mind. Visions of him, no pants, strutting through the department store, should be hilarious. Instead, I have to take a long sip of my iced tea, so I can cool down the inferno of lust engulfing my brain. Only when I'm left with nothing but ice cubes in the bottom of my cup do I attempt an answer.

"Um ... no?"

A dark rumble of a laugh precedes him just before he steps into view. I'm disappointed to find him fully clothed.

"What do you think? Do I look like a teacher?" Nathan

holds his arms out while performing a three-hundred-sixty-degree turn.

When he texted me, asking for my help shopping, I thought it was a joke. But Nathan insisted he was serious. Apparently, in the fall semester, he'll be starting to visit actual classrooms. Which means he needs to dress in something other than his normal jeans and T-shirt combo.

I assumed I was going to hate professional Lucifer. I've never been one to go for the preppy type even if I do enjoy sporting a variety of blazers on occasion.

But I shouldn't have doubted my former nemesis's ability to transform any outfit into an attractive shell for his tempting form.

He's got on a green-checkered shirt, tucked into a snug pair of khakis, with a dark leather belt wrapped around his slim waist.

And he looks fucking hot. The bastard.

"Where are your elbow patches? Any serious teacher has to have elbow patches." Even as I joke, I stand up to push him toward a mirror.

Standing side by side, we're nowhere close to being a matched set. Nathan in his professional attire and me in my cutoff T-shirt, which has a rendering of the periodic table on it. At least I'm wearing a skirt today. But it reveals part of my rib cage and ends only halfway down my thighs, which makes me hardly any more presentable.

Good thing I don't care what the world thinks about my clothes. At my future job, it'll all end up under a lab coat anyway. The biggest concession I'll have to make is wearing pants. Not the best idea to handle chemicals with my legs exposed.

"You're thinking of professors. Teachers, especially elementary school teachers, just need something they can get stains out of and move around in." He tugs on a sleeve and then fiddles with the top button.

"Okay then, can you move around in it? Let's see some squats." I back up, giving him room.

Nathan's one eyebrow arches high. "You just want to admire my ass in these pants, don't you?"

"What?" I sputter. "That's ridiculous. I'm trying to be helpful."

"Oh, really?" That eyebrow is still curved in mockery, and with an evil grin, he does a few lunges, holding my eyes all the while. "Is this what you want?"

"Those aren't squats," I mutter, retreating back to the pleather chair I was perched on before he demanded my input.

When Nathan chuckles this time, the decadent sound of it pulses over my skin, and I try to squash my reaction with more tea. Unfortunately, my cup is empty.

Should've ordered a large.

"But, really, Shorty. The clothes. Are they okay?"

I meet Nathan's eyes and get a glimpse of seriousness behind the laughter.

This means something to him. Of course it does. He wants to do well at a job he loves.

Suddenly, the fact that he asked for my help with this sets a heavy weight on my heart. A pressure that should be uncomfortable, but instead, it carries a sense of being grounded. Of mattering.

"You look good. But I think the shirt might be a size too big. Let me grab you a smaller one." I escape from the dressing room, losing myself in the racks of clothes, so I don't have to figure out my sudden urge to kneel down and propose to the guy I've kissed a handful of times.

When I reach the stacks of shirts, I grab the size I think he needs, and then because it catches my eye, I pick up a short-sleeved crimson button-up with tiny black dots evenly scattered over the fabric. The color combo hints at a devilishness that's perfect for my Lucifer.

No. Not *mine*.

Normal, not mine Nathan.

"Hey, I got you the smaller size. And I want you to consider this other one," I call out as I walk back into the fitting area, juggling the clothes and my cup because there are no trashcans in sight.

"Cool. Bring them in." His voice filters through the door again.

I have to take a second to process what he just said. Maybe I misheard him.

"You mean, hand them to you?" It's the only logical conclusion, so I rise up on my tiptoes to slide the shirts over the top of the door.

But he doesn't grab them.

"No, I meant, bring them in the room. I need your help."

"With what? Did you forget how to dress yourself?" I retract the shirts and rest my hand on the doorknob. Still, I hesitate.

Nathan chuckles. "Maybe. You'll have to come in to find out."

That offer is too tempting to ignore. The latch gives a little welcome click as I crack the door open and slide myself inside.

Since we're the only ones in the men's department, Nathan has commandeered the largest dressing room. When I go shopping, these little spaces become a war zone of tried-on and discarded clothing, resembling the detonation of a trendy clothing bomb.

A sense of camaraderie engulfs me in a comforting hug at the sight of a similar trail of destruction Nathan left in his wake. Shirts hang halfheartedly from hangers or sit in haphazard piles on the bench and floor. Pants are flung over every available surface.

The only thing empty of clothing is his body.

"So, I was right. You did forget how to dress yourself." That was supposed to sound flippant, but instead, I choked on the words and probably drooled slightly.

To be fair, he's not *completely* naked. Nathan still has on a pair of black boxer briefs. They would have to be black, wouldn't they? He couldn't wear some goofy pair of underwear with a cartoon character that we could both laugh about.

Nope. Lucifer has to show me his pale, sexy body with just a scrap of naughty black covering his important bits.

His legs have a coat of dark brown hair. Not werewolf territory, but the guy obviously isn't on the swim team. Too much drag. There's also just the barest hint of fuzz on his chest, enough to make me think about wrapping my arms around his waist and burying my nose in the spot. I already know the way he'd smell. Apple cider, heavy on the cloves.

Can I take a sip of him? Pretty please?

"It's not so much that I forgot"—he saunters across the carpeted floor—"just that I wondered if you might want a peek."

"A peek?" I might as well be Minnie Mouse with how high my voice just came out.

"Yeah, Shorty. You seemed distracted out there. Thought I'd clear up any questions you had about what was going on underneath all these outfits." The devil smiles at me.

If I were more practiced in the arts of flirting and seduction, I might be able to come back with a witty line. Instead, I murmur, "Well, now, I'm going to be even *more* distracted."

He laughs, clearly enjoying the admiration I'm finding impossible to hide.

"Sorry"—he doesn't sound sorry—"thought I was helping. Guess I'll put one of those on."

But when Nathan reaches for the shirts in my arms, I reflexively clutch them to my chest.

"Shorty? Wanna hand them over?" There's a second question lingering under that last one.

Or do you prefer me like this?

"Well, I mean, I just ..." There's no polite reason not to give him the clothes. All that's got me playing keep-away is the craving to continue staring at his bare body just a little bit longer.

Then, he has to go rest his long-fingered hands on his hips, practically directing my eyes to trace over the natural V-shape of the muscles pointing to the only piece of him I can't see.

"You're biting your lip." The teasing note is missing from his voice. Instead, he sounds fascinated, and he watches me with hunger.

I can't seem to stop, even after he pointed it out. The need to kiss him is so heady that my mouth demands stimulation, and all I can give it is a firm pinch with my teeth.

"Shorty, you either need to give me the shirts and leave this room or I'm going to push you up against that wall"—he points behind my head—"and probably do a lot more than kiss you." Nathan folds his arms across his naked chest, and a thick muscle in his neck tenses as he waits.

I don't need much time to consider.

"Option two, please."

His reaction is instantaneous. I drop the shirts and my empty cup half a second before he has me stumbling backward.

Nathan is everywhere. One hand cradles my face while the other delves under my shirt to spread over the skin on my ribs. He shoves a leg between my knees, so I'm straddling his thigh. The guy's body is an oven, baking me with hot lust.

Then, he's kissing me. However, he doesn't start with my mouth like a normal person. Instead, he draws his lips over the contours of my face. Outlining me and leaving a trail of fire behind as he moves from the corner of my eye to my cheekbone, along my chin, and then up around the curve of my ear.

At the touch of his teeth and tongue fiddling with the silver stud in my lobe, a shock wave rockets down my spine. My thigh muscles tense involuntarily, giving the sensation of me riding his leg.

My hands reach up to clutch his shoulders, and I admire the heated skin under my palms.

"That's right," he whispers in my ear, sending more tremors pulsing through my body. "Hold on to me."

Before I can pick up enough of the scattered bits of my brain to formulate a response, Nathan finally captures a kiss from my lips. He takes it, pulling the caress from me with coaxing movements of his mouth until I'm leaning forward to chase the taste of him.

Where we are doesn't register anymore. I'm adrift, half-conscious, like the few minutes between deep sleep and when I open my eyes in the morning. But instead of the remnants of dreams clouding my mind, the disorientation is a side effect of desire. All that surfaces through the haze is how well I fit against him.

Too soon, he takes away the sweetness, returning to trailing openmouthed kisses. Only this time, he heads south, traveling down my neck and over the ridges of my collarbone. Some of the caresses barely brush my skin, tickling me until I squirm. Then, the next presses hard, as if he were attempting to brand me with the shape of his mouth.

I'd let him.

Once Nathan is kneeling in front of me, he pauses. His grip circles my rib cage now, and in unison, his thumbs trace the skin just beneath the underwire of my bra.

"Can I touch them?"

In response, I lift one of my hands from his shoulder in order to reach behind me and unclip the tiny set of hooks at my back.

Slack granted, Nathan pushes his palms up until they cradle

my perfectly respectable B-cups. His fingers play over my hard nipples, gently stroking across them until I'm ready to beg him to push harder. The inside of my thighs are damp in anticipation.

"I think about these all the time," he groans before nuzzling his face into my chest.

The pose—him on his knees in front of me as he practically tries to bury his head in my cleavage—brings on an interesting combination of humor and protectiveness.

I drag my fingers through his hair, massaging his scalp as I go.

He emits a happy hum, but his grasp abandons my chest. Not that I have time to complain, as his touch drifts up the back of my thighs.

I'm losing track of my own body. *When did my legs get so long?* Each moment, I'm sure he's about to reach the edge of my underwear. But the journey is farther than Frodo's goddamn trip to Mordor.

"Just take them off me already!" At the last second, I remember to whisper.

Nathan's chuckle vibrates against my breastbone at the same time he fingers the fabric under my skirt. Following my command, he tugs them down, sliding them off completely when I lift each of my feet in turn.

I expect Nathan to resume touching me. Instead, he sits back on his heels and stares at the piece of cloth in his hands.

"Are these reindeer?" Fascination coats his question, and I let out a growl of frustration.

Who cares about my bright red underwear even if it is covered in Christmas creatures?

Apparently, Nathan does.

"It's April. Why are you wearing sparkly holiday panties?" The guy runs his fingers over them like he's some type of designer examining the quality of the fabric.

"Because they're all like that," I grumble before reaching out to snatch them back.

But he's too quick for me, standing up and backing away, a delighted smile creasing his face.

"You're telling me that every pair of underwear you own has reindeers on them?"

"No!" I punch a fist into my thigh and glare off to the side. "My grandma gives me a gift card to Victoria's Secret every Christmas. So, I go and stock up on the pairs that are on sale, which tend to be holiday ones. I've got snowmen and wreaths and other stuff."

Why? Why do I have to go for the discount table?

"You are"—he pauses mid-sentence, and I turn in time to see him neatly fold my panties and tuck them into the pocket of a pair of jeans I assume he owns—"adorable."

"Adorable?" Not really the adjective I want thrown around right when I'm trying to introduce a hot guy to my vagina.

"Yeah. And"—he pulls out a foil packet from another one of the pants pockets—"sexy as hell."

No longer distracted by my undergarments, I realize Nathan's own are dramatically tented. Seems like he's interested in doing something about it.

In a public dressing room.

His approach is methodical, gaze fixed on me, sauntering like a panther moving toward prey that's already accepted their demise. When he's close enough for his body heat to raise the hairs on my arms, that wicked grin curls across his lips, and he slides the condom into my hand.

He took off my underwear, so I return the favor, stretching the elastic over his erection and pushing it down his thighs until he kicks it off and stands in front of me, bare to the world. It's been a little while, but I don't have any trouble remembering how to pinch the tip of the rubber and roll it down his hard length. The muscles in his stomach twitch and tense in response to my touch.

"Okay, Shorty"—he leans down to place his lips next to my ear and rests his hands on my hips—"you ready to climb me again?"

My arms snake around his neck, and he digs his fingers into the meat of my thighs, lifting me up until I can wrap my legs around his waist. The solid wall at my back and the firm body pressed against my front cocoon me. But I don't want to just be surrounded; I want to be filled.

"Best we don't get caught. So, you're going to have to keep nice and quiet for me. Can you do that?" Nathan's whisper brushes the flyaway hairs at the side of my neck, just as there's a slow stroke through the wetness at my core.

All of my insides clench in anticipation, the head of his cock sitting just against my entrance. The moment I nod acts as the go-ahead, and he slides into me.

How could I have forgotten how great sex was?

Maybe because it never felt this good with Derrick.

Nathan raises his head enough to gaze down at me, holding my eyes with the power of his. Each slow thrust of his hips is partnered with an exhale of breath through his nose. That's the only means he has for breathing, seeing as how his jaw has gone tight from clenching his teeth together.

My mind fills with the sight of him in passion, and the tremors starting between my legs race through every inch of me.

Then, like always, the pleasure freezes my vocal cords. All I can do is breathe in the intoxicating apple cider smell of his soap and listen to his heavy panting and drown in the sensations of him moving inside and against me.

But as my silence reigns, Nathan's lips, pressed tightly together, curve in a triumphant smirk. And I know without a glimmer of doubt that he's aware of exactly how lost I am in our moment. He understands how I experience my ecstasy, and it turns him on.

A small earthquake rocks through my body, everything giving a slight shift, and I no longer have both my feet on familiar ground.

This is falling. Movies and TV and books throw that word around to describe how people careen into deep emotions, and I've only ever held a vague understanding. Like how I know, in an abstract sort of way, what it's supposed to be like in outer space. The sensation has been described to me, and I've watched videos of astronauts floating around. But I don't *really* know.

My ex-nemesis uses the addictive nature of his hands and lips and skin, paired with his soul-searching gaze, to reveal what was a mystery to me before.

The realization terrifies me, spiking my adrenaline and pushing me into a gravity-defying orgasm. As I plummet and float, unmoored, Nathan grips me close, acting as my tether.

Then, someone knocks on the door.

16

NATHAN

"Occupied!" I grunt the word out, ready to murder whoever is on the other side of the door.

Right now? They had to interrupt right now?

This was supposed to be my chance to watch Hannah fall to pieces in my arms. Instead, I have to whip my head around and make sure she remembered to latch the lock on the door.

She didn't.

"Sorry, sir! Just wanted to check in to see how you're doing. Everything fitting okay?" The guy's voice is cheery and apologetic, some store employee looking to help the one customer in his section.

When I return my gaze to the sexy package in my arms, it's clear that panic is quickly forcing away any of the desire she was just experiencing.

Can't have that.

"Yeah. It's a"—I shift inside her until I sit as deep as I can go —"perfect fit."

Hannah's eyelids flutter like epileptic butterflies, and her mouth circles into a lovely O shape.

Got her back.

"Good to hear. Well, my name is Michael. Just give me a holler if you need anything."

"Will do!"

Not likely, fucker.

The whole place is carpeted, muffling all footsteps, so I can't be sure if he hangs around or walks back out into the store.

Good thing my girl is quiet.

I lean down to run my tongue around the cute curve of her ear before whispering, "You ready for round two?" I raise my head enough to watch her eyes widen, eyebrows shooting up close to her hairline.

Keep going? Poor girl is too nervous to speak out loud, instead mouthing the words like we're in a silent movie.

Pressing my lips to the soft skin where her jaw meets her neck, I kiss and lick, and then I quietly answer, "I can make you come again. And I wouldn't mind getting off either. Been fantasizing about finishing inside you."

I'm so close to her that I can observe each individual hair rise as goose bumps scatter over her golden skin. The only response I get is a jerky nod and the quicker rise and fall of her chest.

Thank fuck.

Other than her underwear, I haven't taken any other pieces of clothing off Hannah. Her bunched-up skirt hides where our bodies are fused together. This means, it's all about the feel. The tight, slick grip of her around me. The way her plump ass puckers under my grasping fingers.

Wanting to push harder, delve deeper, I release one of her cheeks and brace my forearm on the wall above her head. Now, I can press myself flush against her. I admire the firm swells of her breasts smashed against my chest and the quick, panting breaths that send bursts of heat over my neck. I find I can bring them out of her with each rock of my hips.

Hannah wasn't lying when she claimed to be quiet, but anyone with eyes in their head and nerve endings under their skin could easily discern the way arousal fills this woman to the brim. Every spark of pleasure is present in the quiver of her lashes and flare of her nostrils. No doubt her strong fingers are bruising my skin from clutching me close during her orgasm. I can't wait to admire the marks she left on me and make her cover me in more.

Then, there's the scent of her. As her skin grows hot, it turns into an oven with a pear pie baking inside. Warm and sweet, flooding my mouth with saliva I need to swallow so I can go back to licking her.

Each thrust into her welcoming pussy is sedate yet frantic, the erotic sensation burning through me like slow-moving lava.

The pace might be torturous, but it's getting us there all the same.

When she reaches down to cup my bare ass, her fingers turning into claws of need, I know she's ready. I lean back enough to admire the ecstasy on her face, all the while making sure my pelvis grinds into her clit.

Then, the walls of her grip me tight, clenching and pulsing as her cheeks flush ruddy.

The extra pressure has me at the edge. I bury my face in her neck, inhaling a deep lungful of her delicious aroma. Bringing her down hard on my dick, I forever entwine the scent of candied pears with spilling hot waves into my girl.

Mine.

I have to bite into her shoulder to muffle my groan.

We stay there—me naked, pinning her against the dressing room wall, with her strong legs locked around my waist—for maybe minutes, maybe hours. All I know is, I don't want to let her slide off my body. I never want her to move away from me.

Not in this room, not in a few weeks when the semester comes to an end.

I don't think I'll recover. Hannah is a magnet, and I'm a compass. One moment, I was pointing north. Now, I'm just directed at her. Only problem is, I know distance won't change that.

She's my new north.

A shiver skitters through her compact body, and when I lift my head from where I settled it on her shoulder, I realize the lustful heat has drained from her skin.

Even with it gone, she still wears a lopsided smile with her eyes settled half-open.

Reluctantly, I pull myself back far enough to let her gain her own footing. The short black skirt falls around her thighs, a flimsy curtain covering perfection.

For a moment, she glances around the room, as if searching for something, before giving me back her gaze.

"Where's my underwear?" As she whispers the question, the first words she's uttered since we started fooling around, Hannah places a hot hand on the side of my rib cage to steady herself as she rises onto her tiptoes, attempting to lean in close to my ear.

It's enough to make me want to scoop her up again and try for another round. Unfortunately, I don't have that quick of a recovery time.

I reach down to slide the used condom off my uncooperative dick as I answer, "I've got them. Safe and sound."

She rocks back on her heels, wrinkling her nose and shaking her head at me. "Those aren't yours to keep." Her hushed chastising just makes me grin.

I tie off the condom and search for somewhere to dispose of it. Even though I talked about this kind of hook-up in the past and was the one to initiate things, I didn't really think it through.

I just wanted her so bad that I couldn't imagine leaving this room without making a pass.

And she went for it. My little exhibitionist.

"Give me that." Shorty reaches toward me.

"I'm naked. I swear I'm not hiding your panties on me."

"No. The condom. Here." She bends over, grabs her soda cup, and pops the lid off before offering it as a makeshift receptacle.

"Look at that." I drop in the evidence of our sneaky liaison. "Teamwork!"

"Keep your voice down!" she whisper-yells at me, even as a grin threatens at the corner of her mouth.

"Why? I'm supposed to be in here. You're the rule-breaker." I have to dodge fast as she tries to pinch my side, chuckling and batting her hand away.

"And what kind of friend would you be if you gave me up? Now, get dressed while I toss this. You still need to try on that smaller size." Hannah cracks the door open to peer out and apparently finds the coast clear because she makes her escape without a backward glance.

Which might have been better because most of my giddiness evaporated at her use of that one word.

Friend.

Not that being her friend is a bad thing. It's just not the only thing I want to be. Friends come and go in your life. It stings a bit to leave them behind, but you get over it.

I don't know how to hold on to her.

What can I do to make her stay?

Because right now, she might as well be a handful of sand slipping through my grasping fingers.

17

———

HANNAH

"You're cheating."

I grin smugly to myself, seeing as how Nathan can't see me. "You were the one who wanted to sit like this."

"Yeah. Sit. You, madam, are not sitting. You're squirming. And very suggestively, too, I might add."

A snicker leaks out, even as I bite down on my lips to try to keep it contained.

We're on the floor of Nathan's dorm. He's got his back propped up against the couch, and I'm tucked in between his legs. This means he has to wrap both his arms around me and hold the gaming controller in front of the two of us. For him, the position has to be kind of awkward.

But as I said, it was his suggestion.

"I think you just can't handle that I'm getting better at this than you."

Friday nights no longer consist of me reading alone in the library. Now, they're all about hot chocolate and Mario Kart. And sex. Which tends to happen first because the second we're alone together and near a bed, Nathan starts kissing me like he's drowning and I'm an oxygen tank.

But it's not just Fridays; barely a day in these past two weeks has gone by without us at least meeting up for a quick coffee on campus. Not surprisingly, Lucifer always offers to order them.

I should be happy. I should be content.

Instead, whenever one of those emotions threatens to put me at ease, I shrink away from it. If I try to pretend like this silly, easy relationship will last forever, then I'll be putting myself at risk for a massive heartbreak. There are no guarantees, and I can't make a decision about my future happiness just because this guy gives me flutters in my chest.

Three of the universities in New York that I'd applied to sent me acceptance letters. I haven't told Nathan. I also haven't replied to the schools.

But it's the end of the week, and I still have two more to go before the end of the semester. No need to get depressed about it all right now. Might as well enjoy the time I have left with him before I put on my big-girl panties and make the mature decision.

"You've improved a little bit. But you still have a long way to go, young grasshopper." He lets go of the controller to reach under my T-shirt. The light touch tickles, and I writhe in his lap, giggling and protesting but to no avail.

We're wrapped up together, laughing and play fighting, when the front door bursts open, and Nathan's roommate stumbles in with his girl of the night.

Bobby scored well.

The Amazon towers in her heeled sandals, each step causing her hip-length russet hair to sway around her pale, freckled shoulders. I admire the cupid curve of her mouth and how she expertly applied her eyeliner—a skill my unsteady hand has yet to master.

Much of my playful giddiness deflates. Neither Nathan nor

I enjoy hanging around and listening to Bobby's rousing sexual exploits. Guess it's time for me to head home.

"Oh. Hey, guys. This is—"

We don't get to find out if Bobby remembered this one's name tonight because she cuts him off, "Your shirt! Oh my God! I love it." The mystery girl shoves away from Nathan's shocked roommate to crouch in front of me. Pinching the bottom of my T-shirt, she pulls it taut. *"My guardian angel wears a trench coat. That is so great! You're a Supernatural fan?"*

I'm impressed. Not many people pick up on my T-shirt's reference to one of the main characters from my favorite TV show.

"*Supernatural*?" Nathan's curiosity is obvious. "That have a pentagram-sun symbol?"

"Duh. The anti-possession tattoo. You watch it?" The stranger clutches her hands under her chin, looking like a child who's stumbled across a puppy.

"He doesn't." I give Nathan a gentle elbow. "But I think I've rewatched the whole series, like, five times."

"Five times?" The Amazon scoffs. "Girl, you need to catch up! You should join the *Supernatural* Club."

"That exists?"

She has to be kidding. If there were a *Supernatural* Club, I totally would've spotted it on the university's website.

"Well, not officially. We don't need faculty advisers telling us how to binge-watch the fight against evil while consuming massive amounts of junk food." She holds out her hand. "I'm Scarlet."

"Hannah." I return her shake, experiencing a pleasant tingle when our fingers clasp.

"Come on, babe," Bobby practically whines, his body leaning toward his bedroom.

"For Pete's sake, just give me a second. Can't you see I'm

making a new friend?" Scarlet leans in close to mutter, "Guy can't even wait a few minutes for high-quality pussy."

Behind me, Nathan chokes on a laugh, and my cheeks turn cherry-red hot.

"Do you like rock climbing?" Her question comes out of nowhere, the wild tracks of her mind harder to stay on course than Rainbow Road.

"Um, I don't know. Never tried it."

Clearly not afraid of personal space, Scarlet grasps one of my biceps, giving a light squeeze, and then clasps my hand again to trace the pads of her fingers over my palms. "You got some muscle, girl. And calluses. You lift weights?"

"A few times a week."

"Well, a little upper-body strength is all it takes. You should come to the rock wall in the gym tomorrow around two. My roommate, Callie, and I'll be there. We can show you how. And quiz you on your knowledge of Sam and Dean Winchester— aka the hottest men on television."

Her grin is almost manic but in a familiar way. It's the expression that arises from the joy of discovering someone else who shares your fandom. My face is probably forming into something similar.

And because I get a kindred sense from Scarlet, I take a risk, praying I'm not shooting myself in the foot. "I'm actually more of a Castiel fan." I name one of the other characters from the show, an angel with floppy, dark hair and soulful eyes.

Scarlet glances at Nathan, likely picking up some of the subtle resemblance between him and my fictional crush. Her grin adopts a knowing edge that shoots up the heat factor in my face a couple more degrees.

"I'm sure you do. Well"—she abruptly stands, towering above the two of us in her massive heels—"you're still invited. Two p.m. Rock wall. Be there, ass-butt."

Nathan stiffens against my back, obviously offended for me.

I, on the other hand, am surprised into a delighted chuckle, easily picking up on her *Supernatural* reference.

Before I can respond, Scarlet saunters down the hall, leaving Bobby to trail in her wake.

When they're gone, Nathan uses his thumb to turn my head to the side, where he can meet my eyes. "Sorry. Didn't know you were going to get ambushed."

"Don't be sorry! She's awesome! *Supernatural* club ..."

My mind skips over all the possibilities. Long discussions about the show. Themed snacks. Friends to share references with.

Sounds like heaven.

"So, you're going tomorrow?" he asks.

"To rock climbing? No doubt. Have you tried it? Is it hard?"

"I haven't. But we both know you're pretty amazing at climbing things." Lucifer's grin turns wicked right before he leans down to press a warm kiss to my lips.

18

HANNAH

"You're a natural!" Callie holds up her plastic dining hall cup to toast me.

I grin at Scarlet's roommate, trying not to preen under the compliment.

If I'd had any worries about intruding on their climbing time, that was immediately squashed when I showed up at the wall. Scarlet cheered at the sight of me, and Callie gifted me with a smile while she clasped the hand of a lanky blond guy. I was quickly introduced to both her and Walter, an employee at the rock wall, who's also Callie's boyfriend.

Since I joined them, their numbers were finally even.

"She's right. I don't think I was brave enough to go all the way to the top my first time around. You've got some steel ovaries." Scarlet taps the back of her hand against my stomach. Little joyful-friendship sparks scatter through my body at the contact.

"You *have* to join our bouldering team next semester. Our fourth bailed at the last minute, and even though Scarlet,

Walter, and I kicked ass, we didn't have a high enough combined score to take home the win."

Black curls escape a tight knot at the top of Callie's head, and Walter absentmindedly fiddles with them as he sits with his arm around her shoulders.

My eyes catch on the movement, and a bit of longing tugs at my heart. Not because I'm interested in Walter. Only because I'm wondering where Nathan is and how much longer I'll get the chance to experience his little gestures of affection.

To keep my mind off those thoughts, I focus back on the conversation. "What's bouldering?" All this foreign terminology has me feeling like I'm learning a new language.

"It's where you climb without ropes. But only to a certain height. Not all the way up the wall," Scarlet speaks as if only half her mind is on the conversation. She stands up from her chair, scanning the crowd of students who are milling around the dining hall, carrying plates piled with pizza and fries.

"And they tape off certain routes. So, you have to use the same holds as your competitors to get to the same place," Callie chimes in.

"Sounds like fun."

Today's excursion, paired with the possibility of more in the future, has my blood pumping with excitement. This must be what Nathan experiences when he shows up at the preschool to help those kids out.

"What're you doing tonight, Hannah? FYI, the right answer is, hanging with your two new friends and watching *Supernatural*." Scarlet is still focused elsewhere, even as she gestures between herself and Callie. Seems she's mastered the elusive ability of multitasking.

It's silly, but her offer makes me want to cry.

Happy cry.

Friendship often seems like a simple thing, but when you go for a long stretch without it and then someone starts to incorporate themselves into your life, the joy of the connection is indescribable.

"Yes. Definitely."

"Am I invited?" Walter hooks his foot around Callie's chair, sliding her closer until she's almost in his lap.

"Oh, sweetie. I love you, but no. No boys allowed. I can't have you stifling me as I lust after a fictional man." She kisses both his cheeks as he rolls his eyes.

The exchange, while adorable, is also extremely comforting. Alexis would never choose to hang out with me over spending time with her boyfriend. It's one of the reasons we barely talk other than a passing hello when we're both in the apartment. That Callie is willing to make time for other people gives me hope that this could turn into a real friendship.

"Hey! Hey you!" Scarlet yells, making me jump.

Callie and Walter don't even flinch, so I guess they're used to her shouting randomly.

A whole mob of heads turns our way, but Scarlet gives them all a frustrated *I'm not talking to you* wave.

"You! Hannah's boy toy!"

Oh shit. My face explodes in a heated blush when I realize the person Scarlet is shouting at is none other than Nathan Cooper.

He stares at Scarlet from his spot in line, confusion dipping his brows until his eyes trip over to me. Then, a wide grin splits his face, and he lifts a hand in a wave.

I'm barely able to manage one in return, mortified at the amount of people staring at our group.

"Yeah, we're over here! Come sit with us when you have your food!" Scarlet waits until he gives her a thumbs-up, and then she settles back into her chair and picks up her fork with a satisfied smile. "So, since Hannah is joining us for the first time, we have to start with season one," the redhead talks as if she didn't just announce to the entire dining hall that Nathan is my human plaything.

And I think I'm realizing that this is something I'll need to get used to with Scarlet as my friend.

Embarrassing but worth it.

Also, when Nathan approaches our group, grin still in place, I find myself grateful for her high-handed ways.

He leans down to whisper, "Hey, Shorty," in my ear before settling in the chair beside me. "How was climbing?" This he says louder, offering the question to the table.

"Great. Hannah is now officially on our bouldering team. This is Callie and Walter," Scarlet explains, and the couple smiles at Nathan. "And this is ..." She lets the sentence trail off, and I realize she didn't call him my boy toy for no reason.

"Nathan," I say.

"Hannah's boyfriend," Nathan adds.

And once again, I'm blushing.

"Good to meet you. I've been needing backup." Walter salutes Nathan from his spot across the table.

"Oh, hush. Callie and I let you win almost five percent of the arguments we have. Stop being so dramatic." Scarlet glares, her arms crossed.

"*I'm* dramatic?"

Walter and Scarlet proceed to bicker in a good-natured way as Callie laughs and throws out comments every so often. Not to calm them down, but instead to keep them going.

I lean back in my chair, glancing to the corner of the room. There's a small table by the window that gets decent light. It's the table I always eat at, sitting alone, reading my book. I don't hate that table, and I don't even hate the idea of eating alone. I'm sure I'll do it plenty in the future.

It's only that today, finally, I have a choice. I have a group.

I have friends.

Under *this* table, a warm hand snakes into my lap. Nathan's gaze stays focused on the verbal volleys being batted around across from us, but from the way our fingers tangle together, I know at least part of his attention is on me.

He leans over, pressing his lips to my ear again. "I like them. Let's keep them."

My cheeks ache as a smile dominates my face.

This whole situation brings on a wave of giddy joy so strong that I want to kick myself.

Why did I give up so easily on making friends?

Okay, so I had a few duds. But it was stupid of me to let myself think there weren't any great people just waiting to be found.

Who knows how much earlier I would have met Scarlet, Callie, and Walter if I had just put myself out there?

How many more potential friends are on this campus right now?

All I need to do is challenge myself once in a while, and I might find a few.

Maybe staying in Virginia wouldn't be so bad. Maybe I wouldn't be all alone if a certain devilish chair thief ever decided to break my heart.

As I glance to my side and meet his laughing eyes, my doubts about us begin to fade away, too.

———

NATHAN

We didn't have any plans last night, so it's not like Hannah technically ditched me to hang out with her new friends, but I get panicky when I think of all the minutes I've lost with her. Those minutes are limited because she hasn't decided to stay.

Today's mission: change Hannah Small's mind.

I smirk to myself when I think of her last name. Can't believe she was able to hide that from me for so long even though I completely understand why she might have thought I'd use it against her. She's a treasure trove of secrets I want the chance to explore.

When I round the red brick corner of the dorm building, I catch sight of Hannah. She's perched on the half-wall where I first got to taste her caramel-sweet lips. There's never going to be a time I'll walk past this spot and not have that memory. If she leaves me, there's still going to be phantoms of her all over campus. Whenever I study in the library, grab a cup of coffee, or sit on the couch in my dorm room, she's going to be there, smiling through a scowl and slipping her pear-scented hair behind the cute curve of her ear. Sleeping in my bed will be torture after having her poised over top of me, biting her lip in ecstasy, the salty taste of her on my fingers.

My plan *has* to work. I need her to stay with me.

Today, she's got on her trademark shorts with a tank top tucked into their high waist. As I approach, the words on her shirt become legible, and my worries temporarily get pushed to the side at the goofy message.

"*Science: it's like magic but real,*" I read aloud, enjoying the way her head pops up in momentary surprise before a pleased grin creases her round cheeks.

"You got it. I'm basically in wizard training right now. Although I'm not sure having a bachelor's in witchcraft is what employers are looking for on résumés." She hops down from the wall and skips over to me, her flip-flops making loud snapping noises as they smack the bottom of her feet.

Hannah doesn't wait for me to bend down to her level, instead choosing to grab a handful of my shirt and dragging me downward into the paradise of her kiss. Her eager mouth doesn't care that we're in public, nor does her wicked tongue as she teases me with it. By the time she releases her hold, I'm practically cross-eyed and panting, wondering where the closest semi-private area is that I can sneak her into.

But my brain hits the restart button and reminds me I have a mission to complete.

Convince Hannah to stay.

Then, we can christen the dorm building stairwell.

"Your distraction tactics, while impressive, won't work, Shorty." I do my best to glare down at her grinning face, which shows not an ounce of remorse.

"Oh, really? I'll just have to try harder next time." She links her hands behind her back and rocks up on her toes. "So, what's the plan today? What's this big surprise?"

Maybe I shouldn't have hyped it up so much, but I've been scrambling for something to get her to stick around. To take a chance on me.

"I can't just give it away. You'll have to blindly follow me."

"Sounds dangerous." Hannah hooks her arm around my elbow. "I'm down."

Please let this work.

As we stroll through campus, the two of us linked together, the shadow of dissatisfaction lingering in the back of my mind —which I've never wanted to admit exists—dissipates. Listening to Hannah recount her girls' night might as well be a practice in meditation because all the muscles in my body ease. My mind hovers in a happy fog of contentment.

She's my girl. I'm part of a pair. It's her and me, no longer against each other, but moving in tandem.

Does she feel it too?

"You're taking me for pie? I love this surprise." Hannah hugs my arm against her chest as we cross the street to pull open the front door of Slice 'Em Up.

A tiny golden bell rattles, announcing our entrance. My date's perfume mingles with the other syrupy fruit dessert scents, making this visit almost an erotic experience.

"I am taking you for pie, but that's not the surprise."

The shop isn't too crowded. We've arrived before the post-lunch rush. Shorty and I pretty much have the place to ourselves, so I pull her to a stop before we reach the counter. Her rubber soles squeak on the blue-and-white-tiled floor.

"You've been feeling like you don't belong here, right? That's why you want to leave?"

As we stand, facing each other, I hold both of her hands in mine, and she playfully swings them, rocking each like two hammocks in the wind.

Hannah's mouth opens as if she's about to answer me, and then she closes it. She starts again, curiosity clear in the way her eyebrows crease. "Yeah ... basically."

"Well, I have definitive proof that you *do* belong here. Come take a look." I beat away all the doubts about my idea and just decide to go for it. There's no room for hesitation or second-guessing if I'm going to get Hannah to stay.

Slice 'Em Up reveals their delicious options by putting them inside a large glass display case. Silver stands hold all manner of pies—apple, cherry, key lime, chocolate, banana. I could go on for a while.

Halfway down the middle row, in the exact center, I spot the caramel pear. Or at least, that used to be how they referred to it. Today, the paper label has another name in swirly script.

The Hannah Smalls.

"That's my name. In front of that pie." Her voice comes out robotic as her fingers press against the glass.

"Yep." I'm trying not to take her lack of reaction as any kind of sign. "And it's not just for today. That's forever. Until the end of time, that is officially The Hannah Smalls. Now, you tell me, would someone who doesn't belong here have a pie named after her?"

The owner of the shop, Maggie, who I got to know really well yesterday, pretends to read a receipt up at the register, but I catch her watching us out of the corner of her eye. She's almost as emotionally invested in Hannah's reaction as I am at this point.

"What? How? I'm pie? I'm a pie?" There's a hint of something in her voice. Maybe something good.

"You're a pie."

At my confirmation, Hannah finally stops staring through the glass and instead gazes up at me. "How'd you do it?"

Knowing she's still within hearing distance, I throw my thumb over my shoulder to point at the shop owner. "You see, Maggie and I know each other. Her son, Oliver, is in Kid Kare. I might have promised her a few free nights of babysitting in exchange for this little favor."

The woman bustles over to us, beaming. "Well, it's not like I took much convincing. You're Oliver's favorite. Besides, I'm a sucker for a grand, romantic gesture." Maggie reaches into the case and slides a hearty slice of The Hannah Smalls onto a plate, setting it on the counter for us. "And did he tell you the best part?"

Mute, Hannah shakes her head.

"He's covered all your future Hannah Smalls slices. You never have to pay for a piece of yourself again!" The grinning woman claps her hands together.

I've only spared half my attention for the shop owner. Sweat beads under my collar as I wait for some kind of reaction from Shorty. Maybe a *thank you*? Or a chuckle? Even a small smile would work.

Instead, I get shouted at.

"You made me a pie!" Shorty wrenches her hands from mine and then proceeds to launch herself into the air in order to wrap her arms around my neck. "I love pie!"

I catch her, holding her against my chest as she slings her legs around my waist and peppers my face with kisses. The embrace radiates with joy, and most of my unease evaporates.

But I still need one questioned answered.

"So ... since you're a pie ... will you consider staying?"

Other ideas, ways to convince her Virginia and I deserve a second chance, begin to form in my mind.

"I'll stay."

My thoughts stutter to a halt for a moment. As I try to come to terms with getting my way, Maggie applauds in the background, and Hannah laughs in my arms.

"Really? You'll come back next semester?"

She nods, and the tension in my chest evaporates.

"Now, put me down, so I can eat a slice of me!" She practically bounces when I set her on her feet. "I bet I'm delicious."

Hannah gives Maggie a thank-you before picking up her piece of pie, grabbing two forks, and settling down at a table.

I follow along behind her, pulling the second chair around so I can sit with my thigh pressed against hers, my arm resting behind her back.

Then, I lean in close enough to smell the pear scent that is all Hannah and brush her long black hair behind her ear, so I can whisper to her, "I look forward to having a taste of you every single day."

Her dark eyes glitter with mischief as she grins and holds a forkful of pie to my mouth. "Bite me."

19

———

HANNAH

"Where are you going? We still have three more chapters!" Carl's eyes are full of panic as I stand up from the table.

"Keep your shorts on. I'll be right back." I do my best to smile reassuringly and leave most of my stuff with him, so he knows I'm not trying to bail in the middle of our study session.

Carl doesn't seem to realize how happy he made me when he asked me to be study buddies for our Chemistry final.

I don't know if Nathan was right about my classmate having a crush on me, but I do know I've added another friend to my slowly increasing social group.

No way am I abandoning him. However, I just saw a tall, rumpled, handsome education major stroll through the library's lobby, and I have some news he needs to hear.

The paper in my hand crumples slightly as I grip it. Even though I get the urge to sprint after him, knowing he's going to reach The Chair before I do, I keep to a sedate pace. Doesn't matter if I get there before him when I promised Carl I'm coming back.

When I round the corner, Nathan is just lowering himself into the cushy leather. His eyes skim over the room and crease at the corners with his smile when he spots me. That mischievous smile turns into a smirk, and he waves a finger at me.

"Not this time, Shorty. I beat you here, fair and square."

I let him revel in his triumph for only a moment as I skip up to his side. "Look how quickly you forget. Trying to weasel your way out of a promise?"

His lips drop to a frown as his eyes remain curious. "What promise might that be?"

"I seem to remember a certain Friday night where I was completely happy, reading in this very chair, when you rudely interrupted me." I perch on the armrest, wearing a smirk of my own. "Now, my tricky Lucifer"—I comb my fingers through his messy hair, affectionately toying with him as he tries to appear grumpy—"do you recall how you got me to abandon my seat?"

He grumbles a word that sounds a lot like *yes* and then reaches to pick up his bag, ready to shift his ass out of my rightful throne.

The pout on his lips is too cute. Before he can stand up, I bend over to steal a kiss. Only, normally, when you steal something, the goal is to get in and get out fast. But I can't seem to retreat. Instead, I linger, leaving myself vulnerable to his grabbing hands. Nathan drags me off my perch and into his arms. For some time, we sit, wrapped up together, our mouths exploring one another.

It takes me a moment to wade through my lust fog, mainly because Nathan is kissing me like I'm hanging off a ledge and his lips are all that's keeping me from plunging to my death. That desperate passion is what reminds me of the paper in my hand.

He doesn't seem ready to give up anytime soon. Reluctantly, I pull back and cover my mouth with my hand before he can dive back in and lull my mind into distraction.

"Pause!"

Nathan gazes, unfocused, at my hand before dragging his eyes up to me. "Pause?"

"Yes. Pause. I need you to hold off on kissing me and read this." I shove the paper in between us.

He slides it from my grasp and peers down at the typed words. After a moment, Nathan skips his stare up to me, one eyebrow curved up in question. "It's a class schedule."

"Yep." I lean forward to see the text and point out the name on the top of the sheet. "It's *my* class schedule. For next semester."

Nathan doesn't respond right away. We sit quietly—him engrossed in the paper and me locked on him.

His silence makes me itchy.

Maybe I misjudged Nathan's feelings. Maybe the pie was just a silly joke rather than a grand, romantic declaration. Maybe the heartbreak is going to happen sooner than I thought.

"You're gonna lose on Wednesdays."

"Huh?"

When Lucifer raises his head, his face almost splits in half from the jaw-cracking grin he's wearing.

"Your Wednesday class. It ends a half an hour after mine. Better say good-bye to The Spot because this sucker is mine." Nathan cackles evilly, and I laugh along with him while pretending to shove him.

"Dream on, Lucifer. I'll use every weapon in my arsenal to defeat you."

He tosses the paper to the side and catches my hands against his chest. "I might be convinced to give it up. But you'll have to be *really* nice to me."

My retort is cut off when he tilts his head to place a hot, openmouthed kiss on my neck. I expect him to keep on with his *inappropriate for the library* caresses, but instead, he grips my hair, gently wrapping it around his wrist and holding me inches away.

"You're staying? For real?"

All joking is gone from his expression. Instead, I see the same vulnerability that lurks deep in my chest reflected in his face.

"I belong here. Sorry it took me so long to realize it."

EPILOGUE

NATHAN

Five Months Later

For someone who got so pissed off at me for falling asleep in this chair, Hannah doesn't seem to have any issues with taking a nap herself.

Not that I'm complaining.

It didn't take us long to realize that the chair was actually big enough for the two of us if I sat down first and Hannah sprawled herself across my lap. Which is how we're set up this Wednesday evening. I have my book propped on her knees, and the notes she was reviewing have slid out of her slack fingers onto the floor. I'd scoop them up if I could do it without waking her.

But I'm happy to let her sleep.

When she's draped over me like this, every piece of me settles. Even though Hannah told me she was coming back in the fall, there was a small, evil voice lurking in a dark corner of my brain that wondered if she might have said that just to get me off her case.

But she wasn't lying. She left New York yet again and showed up on move-in day, just like all the other students. And I took her out for a slice of her pie.

Hannah shifts in her sleep, pressing her nose into my neck and tucking her hands against my chest.

With the soft cushions cradling my back, the cool breeze blowing in from the open window, and her warm body acting as the softest of blankets, the comfort level has reached maximum potential.

Studying is officially impossible.

Carefully, so as not to wake her, I shut my book and let it drop to the floor, where it can befriend her forgotten notes.

I let my muscles relax and my brain go unfocused, and I sink into the magic that is Our Spot.

ABOUT THE AUTHOR

Lauren Connolly wants to live in a world full of happy endings where female pleasure is celebrated, and men are free to experience and express their feelings. She'd also like a world where people can use whatever pronouns they feel comfortable with and fall in love with whoever their hearts desire. The real world doesn't always subscribe to these rules, which is why Lauren often finds herself dreaming up fictional ones.

When Lauren is not writing she is lying about how many fur babies live in her apartment, teaching herself how to sew seasonal throw pillows, or sipping a Moscow mule while scanning multiple streaming services for the best romantic drama series. Do you know what it is? Please tell her because she *needs* to know.

ALSO BY LAUREN CONNOLLY

Contemporary:

You Only Need One

Rescue Me (Forget the Past #1)

Only One Bed: A Steamy Romance Anthology

Paranormal:

Remembering a Witch